AUTHOR ACKNOWLEDGEMENTS

In writing this novel, there are many people who have helped, encouraged and inspired me. First let me thank Brian Henry for his writing classes, critiques and general support. He can be found at Brian Henry Quick Brown Fox (quick-brown-fox-canada.blogspot.com).

Also through those writing classes, my thanks to the wonderful colleagues and writers I met along my path.

I also thank my daughter, Hollie Marie, for her ongoing support and inspiration.

Last, but certainly not least, I credit my two black cats. Constant companions on my desk, who loved walking over the keyboard and waiting for pages to spew out of the printer.

1

Mustang Sally,
WILSON PICKETT

My name is Diana Darling, and I'm a private investigator. I'll admit to the ink still being a bit wet on the printed certificate from my online private investigator (PI) course. I knew there was still office set-up that needed to be done, but I had just landed my first case.

It was exactly 1:30 p.m. on Thursday, and I was in hot pursuit of a vehicle, following the guidelines from my PI manual. Let me rephrase that. It wasn't actually hot pursuit—more of a casual drive whilst I tried to follow the car. Okay, so maybe I ran a couple of red lights, weaving through the traffic. Not like I did it all the time though. At least I put my signal light on, unlike most of the other drivers. Sometimes rules needed to be followed.

Besides, being a private investigator wasn't exactly rocket science, was it? The underarm sweat marks on my new white blouse from Wally Mart belied my inner confidence. A once crisp collar surrounded my now perspiring neck in a limp chokehold.

I gripped the wheel more tightly than I needed to and checked my rear-view mirror more often than necessary. Okay, so maybe I was a tad nervous.

At any rate, the car was easy to spot. You'd have to be blind to miss the vintage 1967 blue Mustang convertible, with its long snout-shaped hood and short deck behind. It was like a sex magnet on wheels; one with a really good engine and staying power. Attributes that most of the men I'd met as of late were definitely lacking.

In the midst of compact cars, vans, and other non-descript vehicles on Lakeshore Road, even a stretch limousine with a full police escort would have paled in comparison. Sunlight ricocheted off the polished bald pate of the driver. He may as well have had a helicopter beacon targeting his head. All I had to do was stay two to three car lengths behind and follow the sunlight.

A quick mental review of chapter four from my online course reminded me of all I needed to know about tailing a suspect's car. I'd aced the test for that unit, earning a 95%. But then again, it was on paper, not the real thing. But my ten-year-old faded grey Hyundai was perfect and wouldn't stand out in the current traffic—not a car Baldy would pick up on. Besides, he probably had no idea he was even being followed. Likely had better things on his mind. I just needed to be careful, bide my time, and take a few photos for my client.

Just yesterday, my client, Baldy's wife, called my newly opened office. Had she been there in person, she would have noticed I have no receptionist and no other staff apart from me. I did, however, have an impressive display of chunky computer screens and monitors in the small waiting room area, advertising everything from the weather in Tokyo to the stock market on Wall Street. It was part of my façade, pretending to be well-established and experienced. First impressions are always important, and you only get one go at it. Mind you, if a client sat there too long, they'd realize that all the videos were on a loop, repeating every twenty minutes. But since I was new in the private investigator business, waiting wouldn't be an issue for my clients.

It never occurred to me to ask how Baldy's wife found the phone number for the Diana Darling Private Investigator Agency. I was just happy to land a client. Her name was Isadora LaPorte. "My husband is having an affair. I know it," she'd declared. While her voice sounded shaky and distraught, as if she was holding back tears, over the hand-held receiver, mostly she just seemed angry. From her timbre and word choice, I pictured her to be about fifty-five years old. I envisioned her as she threw herself into the visitor chair across from my new self-constructed IKEA desk. "He married me for my money, and now he's screwing around with some blonde bimbo half his age," she'd sobbed over the phone. "And there's more, he might be trying to poison . . ." Her voice dropped off.

Unsure if it was just a bad phone connection or she being a tad paranoid, I chose to ignore the last bit. After all, I understood her angst. Not because I'd ever had a lot of money, but I'd had a couple of screwed-up marriages of my own, so it seemed like poetic justice for this to be my first case. After she settled, and gave me specifics about her husband and his whereabouts, I assured her the case would have my full attention. She was fine with my fee, even promising to put a cheque with half the amount in the mail today.

I dreamt of jacking up my rates and hoped for more referrals from this soon-to-be satisfied customer. But for now, I was hot on the trail, focused, and mentally adding the rest of the anticipated large bill to my bank account. *Ka-ching*!

...

The stubby rear tail light of the Mustang winked its signal. As the car turned right, I eased off on the gas pedal, not wanting to be too close. As the car pulled into the parking lot of the Whispering Pines motel, I muttered, "Oh for God's sake, could ya not have picked a better place?" The motel was renowned, mostly because it rented rooms by the hour—it was one of those *no tell* motels. To folks in the area, it was also known as the Eager Beaver. Even I knew that, and I was well beyond having sordid affairs in seedy motel rooms. Well mostly, except for the couple of times that I now chose to forget for good reason. The place hadn't changed much since my last visit a few years back. Still had grass that needed cutting, a green sludge over the pool, and rusted deck umbrellas that threatened to be released by a really strong wind.

I found a spot in the rear of the parking lot and sank down in my seat. My chin brushed the middle of the steering wheel as I pulled my Nikon camera from the passenger seat and affixed a long-range zoom lens. My elbow accidentally hit the horn and a loud blast followed. *Crap!* I threw myself across the seat. The gearshift jabbed my side and I cursed. My Timmie's coffee that was sitting in the cup holder was now spewed across the front of my brand-new blouse. Not only was I in pain, I was also a mess. Damn, I may as well have mounted a neon sign, with flashing letters for Baldy, saying: "Here I am! Come and find me."

After what seemed like a decent time to wait, I cautiously peeked over the steering wheel. No one seemed to notice me. I propped the heavy long range lens on the dashboard for stability and carefully avoided contact with the horn. Bring it on, you cheating bastard! Diana Darling is poised and ready for action.

As the suspect exited his car, he took a look around, as if scoping out the perimeter. Possibly my horn shattering the silence had him on high alert, or maybe it was just his guilt related to the sin he was about to commit. It was obvious he knew where he was going. No check-in at the front desk, just a purposeful stride to motel room 69 on the ground floor. Even the number was a cliché. I wondered if they paid more money for that room just because of the number. Then I noticed there was actually a 69A, 69B, and 69C. There was my sign!

What made me smile the most were his flood pants. What self-respecting guy wears pants that show half of his socks? From her voice and dialect, I pictured my client, Isadora, as a classy lady, probably dressed in Bianca Nygard's latest fashions. How in hell she'd ended up with this dude wasn't my problem. I just had to catch him *in flagrante delecto.* Or as chapter seven from my course indicated, *naked and in the act.*

Suddenly, the door to room 69A opened. There stood a blonde woman with a bad dye job that looked as if it had been done by a hairdresser with a hangover. She wore a low-cut crimson top that bared half her jiggling triple Ds, and a pair of black knee-length tights that stretched the limits of spandex. I'm not sure where my client got her information from, but if this lady was half the age of the suspect, someone was seriously amiss on mathematics. She qualified as the epitome of a worn-out cougar. My worth-every-cent-I-paid-for zoom lens exposed her false eyelashes, robin's egg blue eyeshadow that Kresge's discontinued in the 1970s (for good reason), and overdone bright red lipstick that would probably stain only God knew where. Christ, I didn't even want to think about it.

My camera was ready. *Snap, snap, snap.* I caught their game of tonsil hockey, just before they closed the door.

It was a start, but not enough. Damn, I needed to get closer. A deserted cleaning cart was parked about three rooms away on the sidewalk. With brooms, garbage containers, recycling bins, and cleaning supplies, it was a perfect cover. I nudged my car door closed with a hip thrust, not wanting to make any more noise than I already had, then crouched behind the cleaning cart and rolled up to the window of room 69A. Only people walking on the sidewalk would be able to see me, and for now it seemed deserted. The Whispering Pines motel was not a hub of activity at two o'clock in the afternoon. I presumed the lunchtime crowd had already left, after paying the twenty-five dollars per hour, including the two-hour minimum charge.

The curtains to the room were left ajar at the bottom of the window. Opportunity beckoned. All I needed was a shot of naked bodies, for Baldy's wife to pursue her lawsuit. It wasn't illegal to have an affair, and my client knew that. All she wanted were some photos to blackmail her husband and end up with a better divorce settlement. "There's no way that guy is getting half my money," she'd said. "He's a minister. He'll probably just give it all away."

It made me wonder if he prayed at night. Did he follow the commandment about *forgive us our trespasses or naughty things we may have done*? I reckoned this guy had probably broken more commandments than just this one. At any rate, it didn't matter. His vices equated to more money in the bank for me.

I cringed at the thought of seeing Baldy butt naked—not a pretty sight. Surely though, it would be a quick in and out, on all accounts. He didn't seem like the kind of guy to wine and dine his date with flowers or any meaningful, extended foreplay.

Without looking through the window, I switched to a shorter camera lens, positioned the Nikon at the gap in the curtains, and pressed the button. The bed had to be in the middle of the room, didn't it? *Oh well*, I thought, *just enough to satisfy my client and spare me the pain of seeing a naked Baldy.* I tried to snap the photos, but there was no clicking sound coming from my Nikon. The screen displayed a picture of my cat. Shit! I had it in the wrong mode. Didn't the damn camera know what I wanted? I switched it from picture viewing to picture taking, then tried again. Darn, still no shot of his butt doing the dirty. Now there was nothing but a blank screen.

Snap, snap! The sound of a camera from over my head caught me off guard. "Hey, lady, what are you doing?" a man's low-pitched voice whispered into my left ear. Where the freaking hell had this guy come from? He was so close that the scent of Old Spice infiltrated my nostrils and his leg brushed against my knee.

I jumped up and banged into the cart, rolling it off the edge of the sidewalk. *Crash, bang, clang.* My body followed the cart, and I ended up sprawled on the pavement, flat on my back with my legs splayed in the air. Thank God I was wearing pants instead of a skirt. As the front door to room 69A burst open, there stood a semi-naked Baldy, with a towel draped around his waist. Skinny legs with varicose veins and hammer toes met my eye level. The last thing I wanted to do was look up!

"What's going on here?" Baldy shouted.

"I'm sorry, just a mishap with the cleaning lady. We'll be out of your way soon," said the man who had whispered in my ear mere seconds before. His voice was calm and controlled. "Fine. As long as that's all it is." Baldy slammed the door, oblivious to the two cameras now lying on the sidewalk. Mine looked broken and I was pissed.

Still on the ground, I looked up into the grey-green eyes fixated on me. His firm jaw held a hint of a smile, and his crew cut reeked of a cop or someone with a military background. Shit, what had I gotten myself into?

"Maybe next time, you'll remember to take the lens cap off before photographing close-up scenes," he smirked.

I hated the controlled laughter in his voice. I hated that he was helping me to my feet. I hated everything about him. Mostly I hated the fact that I'd missed my opportunity for the photographs.

"It seems like we're on the same case, just from different angles. Here's my card. Call my personal number on the back." And then he was gone.

My first case was a bust. I watched as the stranger walked across the parking lot and entered a black Jeep Cherokee. Nice firm butt in tight jeans. Perhaps about forty-five years old and approximately five feet, twelve inches tall. Part of me wondered if he looked as good coming as he did going.

I gathered up the remnants of my camera lens, tossed them into the conveniently available garbage container, and hastily copied down the licence plate number to his truck. Pleased that some of my detective skills weren't going to waste, I could track him down. That's when it dawned on me. I was holding his phone number in my hand!

2

The Pink Panther Theme,
HENRY MANCINI

It had started out as a mid-life crisis. I was twice divorced, hated my current job as a number cruncher for a government revenue agency, and decided at the age of forty to reinvent myself. If men could do it, so could women. It took me a while to figure out what I wanted to do until a flyer for online courses landed in my mailbox.

Culinary school didn't seem like a good fit, given that I was prone to setting off the kitchen smoke detector while boiling water. And then there was the incident of the stovetop fire involving a grilled cheese sandwich. It had taken me a week to clean up the foamy yellow substance the fire extinguisher had spewed out and left strewn everywhere.

After striking chef off the list, I reviewed Witchcraft 101. Nah, I'd leave that one to my mother. Up until she passed two years ago, she'd been the town witch and local psychic reader. Growing up as the daughter of a witch had been difficult. It seemed no one wanted to date me unless it was Halloween, and that was usually on a bet or dare. Most guys in my high school years were more interested in taunting me or pasting witch hats on my locker. Fortunately, I excelled in math and perhaps that's what led me to becoming an accountant. Besides, numbers and mathematics were more easily explained than witchcraft. Mind you, my mother made a good living at it—enough to raise me on her own. Perhaps that could be Plan B?

My next option was creative writing, with the promise for a speedy cash return on the publication of short stories or novels. That process seemed a tad lengthy, and writing was not my forte, given that I'd barely passed grammar in high school. The same with clothing design—I barely passed the sewing course in home economics. Hell, I couldn't even change the bobbin in a sewing machine without jamming my finger on the needle and leaving a trail of blood.

It was the online course to become a private investigator that caught my eye. But did I have what it takes? Well, the pre-qualifying tests assured me I have the skills and abilities. I read the comments over and over again, just to make sure. "Based on your answers for the test scenarios, you will be a natural. Your scores were off the charts! Given your maturity, current skills, and aptitude, you should be able to create your own private investigator business within three months of completing and passing the assignments."

Wow, I never heard anything positive like this from my previous employer. Mostly, they said I wasn't being productive or efficient enough, or they said that sometimes I spent too much time on coffee breaks. *Sign me up for the PI course*, I'd decided. In just a few weeks, I put out my shingle and launched my new career.

...

As I headed back to my car in the parking lot of the Whispering Pines motel, I was second guessing my decision. Perhaps being a private investigator was more complicated than I'd first thought. Acing the multiple choice questions on the test, with a chance for a do-over if you didn't like your first score, had seemed simple enough. And even paying an extra fifty dollars for the certificate after the final exam was fine with me. It meant I was legitimate and had the paper to prove it.

The owner of the strip mall, where I rented my office, was unaware that I was actually living in the space at the back of the unit. It was a *no no*, and I knew it. Plus, I had a cat and was pretty sure I'd be breaking more than one rule here. My choices included: pay rent for a workspace, pay rent for an apartment, or combine the two. The latter was a go, and I was convinced the owner was kind of like a refrigerator light bulb—useful, just not too bright. I could pull this off, and he would never know. Given my current financial resources, I had six months to make this whole business venture work.

Once back inside my car, my stomach started to grumble. Catching sleazy husbands and colliding with a cleaning cart must have made me hungry. After a trip to the local greasy spoon for a quick snack of fish and chips, I carefully backed my car into the designated spot outside my office. You never know when I'd be called to race to a case. Or so I hoped. Upon opening the door to the Diana Darling Private Investigator Agency, I nearly slipped on a brown envelope that had been tossed through the mail slot. What the hell was this?

There were no postmarks, just a legal-sized brown envelope. My name was written in black marker on the front along with a message. *This is for you. Hope it helps.*

I tore it open and dumped out the contents. Holy crap! Photos of the Blondie with Baldy in all his glory spilled onto my desk. The photos were disgusting, but it was exactly what I needed for my client. The pictures had to be from that guy who interrupted my surveillance. Now, how had he gotten them printed so quickly?

I pulled his business card from my wallet and read the name. *James R. Woods, Private Detective.* I grabbed my phone, memorized his personal phone number on the back of the card, and was about to punch it in. *Wait, stop a minute,* I chided myself. Chapter three from my course discussed collecting information on individuals. He obviously knew who I was. Before calling, I needed to do my own background check on Mr. Woods. I located the course manual on my bookshelf, tossed it onto my desk, and reread the relevant chapter. "Go to your local library and check statistics. There's a lot you can find out about people if you know where to look. Always make the librarian your best friend. They are a valuable resource and a wealth of information."

This sounded a tad dated. Screw the library. I was headed to the Internet: the vast garbage pit of anything and everything that needed to be sifted through. I wasn't exactly a techno genius, and in all honesty, the computer was a formidable opponent. It had taken me a full three days just to figure out how to access the course material online.

After a few false leads and starts, I found him. Wow, I was impressed. James Woods was a twenty-year veteran with the police force, who rose through the ranks and became a detective before opening his own business. At least that's what it said on his website, and it sounded legitimate. I picked up my phone again and dialled his phone number. He answered on the second ring.

"Woods here. How can I help you, Diana?"

I was taken aback. Okay, he had call display—something I needed to work on, even though it would cost more money. "Um, I just wanted to say thanks for the photos." Part of me wanted to hang up after hearing his stifled chuckle over the line. Part of me wanted to ignore his superior attitude. But it was his next words that stopped me cold.

"Diana Darling, I need your help, and I think you're perfect for this."

I was gobsmacked. The words I wanted to speak aloud weren't forthcoming. The brain cells that ruled my logical thoughts were misfiring and refused to connect with my mouth. "Huh?" was all I managed.

"Just a case I'm working on. Do you have any experience with undercover work assignments?"

Yes, I've been under the covers a few times, I thought. Not necessarily work-related, except for the boss I screwed after last year's office Christmas party when I was in a drunken stupor. "Absolutely," I replied.

Did he think I was a hooker? I was about to respond when he interjected.

"It pays well. Part of the money will go to you. It should be around two thousand dollars. I think you're kind of new to the business, and you're exactly what I need."

Two thousand dollars. Holy shit! That would cover my rent for the next three months. Whatever it took, I would do it. As long as there was no sex and no illegal activities involved, I could handle this. "I will require a few more specifics about the case before committing," I replied, tongue-in-cheek.

I wasn't stupid enough to go half-cocked, but the money was a definite enticement. "Name the place and time," I said, pleased with myself for sounding succinct and businesslike.

"Pack an overnight bag, just in case you decide to help me out. I'll be at your office at 1500 hours." James Woods disconnected before I had a chance to ask any more questions. Patience wasn't one of my strong suits. I debated on calling him back, but decided against it. At the very least, thanks to him, I had photos to close my first case. I owed him for that. James had earned twenty minutes of my time, even if it went nowhere.

Now I just had to figure out what time 1500 hours was! He must be working on one of those 24-hour clock systems. Starting at midnight, I added fifteen hours and came up with 3:00 p.m. Perfect! I stripped out of my disastrous white blouse and left it to soak in bleach and detergent in the bathroom sink. Twenty minutes later, I was trying to figure out where to hang it. It wasn't like there was a bathtub or a shower curtain rod in the office. The only option was the coat rack in the front hall, so I made a mental note to collect my blouse first thing in the morning.

3

Oh! Darling,
THE BEATLES

My suitcase was packed. I really wasn't sure what to pack because I had no idea where I was going, or even *IF* I was going. A few casual clothes, a track suit, a cocktail dress (just in case I needed to strut my stuff), my kitty pyjamas, and a bathroom bag. That should cover all the bases. Anything else I needed, Mr. Woods would be buying, and I'd be keeping tabs on that. Besides, he could probably write it off as a business expense. The cocktail dress, a.k.a. the bridesmaid dress, was from ten years ago. Before tossing it in the suitcase, I grabbed a pair of scissors and cut off some of the frilly stuff around the shoulders in an attempt to make it look more sophisticated. It turned out to be pretty decent. Maybe that sewing course wouldn't have been such a bad alternative after all.

The high-heeled shoes, however, were a different story. If the situation required, perhaps I could hit James up for a new pair instead of wearing the ones I dyed pink to match the colour of my dress. I hated those heels, mostly because they squished my toes, and even worse, they made my feet sweat. Plus, the shoes were now a disaster that looked more like a tie-dyed T-shirt. Years later, the colour only somewhat resembled the pink cocktail dress, with a few purple and grey spots that were not originally there. Mmm, I wondered if shoes could get mould on them. I sprinkled the inside of the shoes with baking soda, stuffed them with scented dryer sheets, and tossed them into my suitcase.

I changed the cat litter box and put out extra food and water for my little Xena. She'd be fine without me for two days. I knew that when I got back, she'd be waltzing down the hallway away from me, with her tail straight up in the air—a fitting accompaniment to the overwhelming odour from the litter box. A message that implied: "How dare you leave me?" I adopted Xena, my one-year-old black kitty, from the local humane society, but truth be told, she rescued me. She was my constant companion, sat by my computer while I did my online course, and answered some of the test questions by walking across the keyboard. And made sure I never overslept in the morning by bunting against my head when there was an empty spot in her food bowl. She had trained me to accept that there would be no more sleep for me until it was full of food again. The joke about dogs having owners and cats having staff was a truism where I was concerned.

As for James Woods, I still wasn't sure about him, but the money was too good to ignore. At any rate, I'd hear him out. Worst case scenario, I could bail and never have to see him again. While I waited, I tried to call my client. Her voice mail was full, so I e-mailed her instead, assuring her I had photos that would put her husband in a compromising situation and my final report would be ready for her by Monday.

Meanwhile, the coffee machine burbled, hissed a final sigh, and I pulled two mugs from the desk drawer, not a moment too soon. I watched through my office window as the black Jeep Cherokee expertly slid into the spot beside mine. Mr. Woods definitely looked good coming. He sported an expensive black leather zippered jacket, with dark grey distressed jeans that met his pointed toe cowboy-style boots. No flood pants for this guy. He grabbed a briefcase from the back seat and confidently strode through my office door. Polaroid sunglasses were promptly pushed up on his head. I held back from telling him it wasn't sunny outside, but perhaps that was just his style. For two thousand dollars, I could bite my tongue until it bled. "Nice sign, Diana Darling," he commented. "It looks new."

I made a mental note to brush a solution of water and copper sulphate over the bronze door plate. The sign would instantly age, and my clients wouldn't take me for a newbie, but all that could wait. It was time to get down to the facts. Chapter five from my course was all about intake. I took him to my office, hoped he'd missed my blouse still hanging on the coat rack in the hall, and offered coffee as a diversion.

"So what can I help you with? You mentioned an assignment." I slid a mug towards him, while pointing at the cream and sugar. My intent was keeping the conversation strictly to business. There was no way he'd be getting anything less than professionalism from me.

"First things first, I presume you got the photos from yesterday." He cocked his left eyebrow, and it annoyed me.

"Yah, I got them. It's the reason you're here and I'm listening today."

"Glad I could help you out."

I waited. If he wanted me to grovel, he was out of luck. Sometimes silence is a powerful tool. Let him play his cards, speak first, and then I'd decide about his business proposal. My mouth overrode my brain—something that frequently happened to me. "So you need a woman for two days?" I blurted out.

He grinned broadly. "Let me explain."

I nodded. It was time to shut up and listen.

"I'm following up on a case involving two women and possible links to a third. It relates to a retreat program for couples therapy. Both of my clients claim they were approached in a sexual manner by the male marriage counsellor."

"Okay, so what's the deal?" This was getting interesting. I didn't recall any chapters in my course addressing this particular scenario. Perhaps I could make it up as I went along.

His silence was bugging the shit out of me.

"So do me a favour. Just lay it all out on the table," I said. Crap, I'd just broken my own rule of keeping mum twice in five minutes.

"The counsellor has recorded the women in compromising situations. It's kind of delicate, and my clients prefer to remain anonymous. In the videos, the counsellor's face is blurred."

"And," I prompted.

"He's blackmailing them and threatening to send the video to their husbands, unless they pay him to keep quiet. I need you to go undercover as my wife. There's a couples retreat starting today, and I've reserved a room. I can fill you in on the way there. Are you up for this, Diana Darling?"

He delivered his synopsis like a pro giving a report. There was a hint of teasing in his tone. I ignored it, opting to press further.

"How'd you find me?" There was no way I was letting him think I was some newbie investigator.

"From the last case at the motel. I have to presume your client is the wife of the guy; mine is the husband of the woman who was in the motel room. And, I am a private detective after all."

Damn, it was hard to ignore those charismatic eyes, focusing on me and commanding a flush that crept up my neck and into my cheeks. It was like an instant menopausal hot flash, even though I wasn't quite there yet. Take a deep breath. Compose yourself. Resist the urge to fan your face before responding.

"So it seems like I'll be your pretend wife." Part of me wanted to ask how he knew so much about me, yet my inner thoughts were shrieking. Why look a gift horse in the mouth?

"We'll have two hours en route for debriefing. I'll bring you up to speed on the guy we're investigating. And just know this. I'd never put you in harm's way," James said.

"And I should trust you because?" I asked.

"Didn't I just help you close your first case?"

Damn, he knew it was my first case. How good was this guy?

"You definitely helped me close my most RECENT case. Anyway, I'm good to go," I replied. As far as I was concerned, the deal was done.

He'd already picked up my mauve floral suitcase that was parked by the entrance and headed out the door. "I'll take that as a *yes*," he responded, glancing over his shoulder. "Nice suitcase."

"Makes it easier to find at the airport baggage carousel." I wasn't stupid. Besides, it was another Wally Mart special and only cost me twenty bucks. Though I couldn't help but notice his bag was leather and bore a Swiss label.

I settled into the warm leather seat of his Jeep and focused on the glossy brochures he passed my way. He drove, and I read aloud.

"Welcome to the Seasons Inn. We're here to help. If you're feeling disconnected from your significant other, need reconciliation, or just want to get refocused, we're here for you. Our board-certified therapists are ready to guide you, every step of the way."

I glanced at James and saw him looking at me from the corner of his eye. "Sounds like a touchy-feely kind of encounter. Besides, who gets paid for writing this crap?" Maybe those creative writing classes wouldn't have been such a bad gig after all. Hell, I could have written this stuff in my sleep, and there was probably some kind of spell check on my computer that would correct any grammatical errors.

"Keep reading," he said.

"This intense two-day encounter will help establish and identify goals for couples who may feel disconnected or unfocused. Goals are a way to gain traction towards reconciliation. Mmm," I muttered. "The last time I heard about traction, it was related to tires. Does that mean I'll need the high-test tires? The ones with radial tread?"

James stifled a grin. "Read on, it gets better."

"Individual counselling sessions can be arranged. Your confidentiality is assured," I read aloud. "So what do I need to know before we head into this, James?"

We were stopped at a red light. His grey-green eyes held mine for just a tad too long, and I was starting to fidget. Damn, why did this guy have such an impact on me? I was thankful when the light turned green and he continued.

"My clients said the marriage counsellor would strike when they're most vulnerable. Obviously the couples are attending because of problems in the first place and then he creates a situation for the wife to be on her own with him. "

"Sounds like a real letch! I can't wait to meet him. Serve him up some of his own grief.. Do we have a plan?" Then it dawned on me. "I don't have to get naked with this guy, do I?"

"No, Diana. No naked stuff. Trust me. I'll have your back. We're just going to play along. See if the guy hits on you, get some evidence, and then deliver him an ultimatum to back off of my clients. Besides, I'd never do you no wrong."

The sunglasses were back on his nose, and I couldn't see his eyes. The tweak of his right cheek gave him away. It seemed obvious he was toying with me, and I wanted to let him know that I wasn't a newbie at private investigating. "I'll play your game. However, you will need to pay some extra fees. My camera needs repairs after yesterday's fiasco, and I might need some new high-heeled shoes. I didn't have much time to shop before packing." I held my breath, wondering if he would take the bait.

His eyes wandered to my black Nike knockoffs; the kind where the trademarked slash was upside down. "Size six. Shouldn't be a problem. How about some Jimmy Choos?"

I swooned at the thought. "Sounds perfect," I said.

I could sell the shoes on something called Craig's List and probably secure another two months' rent. This case just kept getting better and better. It also confirmed my decision in selecting the PI course. Wow, I was getting life right!

Ninety minutes later, the Jeep followed a meandering path to the Seasons Inn. Gated doors and mature pine trees lined the road. It was definitely several stepladders up from the Eager Beaver. I knew from looking at the brochures that only part of the inn was designated for the couples retreat. That was fine with me. Maybe I'd have a chance to blend in with the real people instead of the disconnected, antagonistic, and unfocused couples I was prepared to meet in the therapy session.

The concierge met us at the front entrance, standing in front of the gleaming full-length glass doors with not a fingerprint in sight. "Welcome to the Seasons Inn. Let me assist you with your check-in and baggage." He waved his hand, summoning a porter who immediately grabbed my mauve suitcase. Yuck, was he laughing at me?

James seemed to be taking everything in stride. I'd just follow along. After all, he was the one who was paying. There was only time for a quick check of the room to unpack and hang up clothes before we headed off to the introductory session. I was relieved to see a sofa in our room because that's where Mr. Woods would be sleeping. The sofa looked kind of small, and he was pretty tall, definitely five feet, twelve inches, which translated into six feet. But that was his problem, not mine.

4

The Game is On (Sherlock theme song),
DAVID ARNOLD AND MICHAEL PRICE

"Welcome to the Seasons Inn and to the Friday evening session of *how to connect with your spouse*. My name is Andrew. I'm pleased to see some familiar faces. If it's your first time here, let me assure you the experience is one you will never forget. Tonight's exercise is just a brief introduction, and I'll be outlining the direction our program will take over the next two days. Always remember, we're here to help."

The fact that he mentioned familiar faces wasn't lost on me. It made me wonder if the therapy sessions hadn't worked the first time around for some. Maybe it was like one of those coupon things where you register and get a bonus class for free. I filed that in my mental notes of information to share with James.

Andrew was pretty good looking, for an older guy. A tanned face and lean build, sporting a light blue leisure suit. His tone was smooth, polished, and reminded me of a car salesman. Cripes, the last time I'd heard a voice like his, I'd ended up buying the lemon of all vehicles. It was twenty years ago, and I'd been lured in by the salesman's pitch and the cheap price. "Only driven by a little old lady," the salesman said. "Plenty of miles left in this baby." Well, the motor died after two blocks of driving that tin box out of the parking lot, and it cost me a hundred bucks for a tow to the junkyard. Since I hadn't purchased the extra insurance, I was shit out of luck. But I'd learned from my mistakes. I might be new at being a private investigator, but I was bringing my past experiences and life skills along with me.

James and I took our seats in the front row of a small conference room, surrounded by approximately ten other couples. I'd already spotted most of them in the foyer when we checked in.

Other vacationers at the inn were easily identifiable as being there for fun and frivolity. They oohed and aahed over the spa facilities, in-house sports activities, and local wine tasting tours. The married couples were a different story. Mostly it was the husbands with that lamb-being-dragged-to-slaughter kind of look on their faces. Meanwhile, the wives' eyes were filled with hope and promise of better things to come.

But James and I were undercover. I shot him a fleeting glance, pleased to see his face had a kind of dogged expression that read, *I'd rather be anywhere else on earth than in this stinking room.* Role playing seemed to come naturally to him. Following his lead, I opened my eyes extra wide and wore a hopeful smile, as we settled into the plush conference chairs.

Andrew strode across the slightly raised platform. With overdone gestures and intense direct eye contact, he was the consummate snake oil salesman. Smooth, mesmerizing, and hell, I might have been tempted to buy a rust bucket car from him, even though I'd already learned my lesson. James nudged me, as if to say, *keep alert.*

Andrew must have caught our exchange because he zeroed in on us like a hawk seeking prey. "I think you're first-time guests here. Is that correct?" he asked us.

"Ya got that right," drawled James.

Where in hell he'd pulled that accent from, I had no idea. I would play along. After all, that's what I was getting paid for.

Andrew knelt on the stage, directly in front of us. Any closer and he'd have been in my lap. "Would it be okay if I asked a few questions? It's just to give the others a sense of what's to come."

I nodded eagerly, and James grunted in assent.

"Part of our journey here is seeing how well you know each other. It is essential that you know the things that are important to each other." He peered at the stick-on name tag on James's shirt. "So tell me, James. What do you think is your wife's favourite flower?"

"I'd have to guess all-purpose flour because she likes to bake," James replied.

I cringed. There were a few stifled snorts of laughter from the men in the group; a couple of gasps from the women. Andrew gave me a sympathetic look.

"Perhaps a different question would be better," Andrew said. "How about . . . what does your wife like to do in her spare time?"

"Uh," James hesitated. "I dunno, but I think she spends a lot of time couch pressing and watching the soaps. Don't you, darling? But you're always there for me when I get home from work. Supper is always on the table. You're the best." His voice had turned sugary sweet. He leaned towards me and gave me a peck on the cheek.

I gave James my best glare, clearly on display for Andrew to see. "Sure, Jimmie, you know me really well," I said in a loud voice for the crowd, pleased that I'd injected a hint of sarcasm in my tone.

"Ah, yes, I can see we have a lot of work to do, and I'm so happy you've joined our group." Andrew stood up and repeated the same exercise with a few other couples.

James gave me a wink and whispered, "That was perfect, Diana. Just one favour. Don't ever call me Jimmie again."

"Okay, Jim," I sighed. "Andrew's right, we have a lot of work to do. When does it really start?"

"It already has."

We managed to keep a low profile during the rest of the hour-long presentation. Every so often, Andrew made a point of catching my eye. The message was clear. It appeared I'd been targeted. James patted my hand. I took the gesture to mean I was doing well.

I was relieved when we could head to the lounge for cocktail hour. James ordered two martinis, and I settled into the bench seat of a private booth.

"So, Diana, what's your take on the group?"

I was considering my reply when the waiter arrived with our drinks. There sat two very large glasses, dripping with moisture, with tiny green olives served on a plastic skewer. I'd make sure to eat them last. Better to let them marinate.

The first slurp of gin burned my throat, and I felt an immediate rush to my head, quickly followed by a loosening of my tongue. Skipping lunch and drinking almost pure alcohol was like an accident waiting to happen. Suddenly my tongue started flapping though not yet entirely out of control. I struggled to enunciate, then took a deep breath and spoke a tad slower. "Well . . . so far Andrew is coming across as charismatic. His eye contact is intrusive at times and . . . he seemed to do a lot of staring at my chest." Christ, had I just blurted that out!

"Continue, Diana, your observational skills are excellent."

I chose to ignore the hint of amusement in James's voice. "Aside from that, there are six couples who've completed the therapy sessions before and know each other. If you were to look over your shoulder, they're in a group at the bar. Based on their interactions, I'd surmise they may be into spouse swapping. Of the other three couples, two are sitting near the exit, and the last couple isn't here," I said.

My report was concise, but I wasn't finished.

"And just in case you missed it, there are already two women eyeing you from the bar. Don't turn around now because the brunette is staring holes into the back of your head. Sadly, the other prospect is old enough to be your mother."

"Well done, Diana. I knew there was a reason I picked you."

"And just why did you pick me?" I was curious and needed to know. I also was beginning to wonder how in hell he knew so much about me. Maybe I should Google myself and see what comes up?

"Simple," he replied. "Your looks fit the profile on Andrew's track record. Of course, he doubtless picks his targets for their ability to pay. In other words, they have rich husbands."

"Fascinating. Tell me more," I said.

"Well, to begin, Andrew is a felon. He used to go by the name of Dennis Moriarty, and he served two years in prison for fraud. When he was released, he resurrected himself as a marriage counsellor. From my research, it appears he took an online marriage counselling course from some chintzy school in California. You know the kind where you just have to answer the questions, and they mail you a certificate at the end if you decide to pay the fifty bucks. Now he touts himself as being an expert or a guru in the field."

I nearly choked, taking another slurp of the gin instead. My palms started to sweat. All I wanted to do was slide under the table. What would he say if he found out about my course? Not that it mattered. Besides, I was convinced my course was legitimate. He seemed to overlook my physical reaction, and I was relieved when he kept speaking.

"Both of my clients indicated he hit on them during the dinner scheduled for the final evening of the retreat. His pattern seems to be making a connection at dinner and then enticing them to meet him in a hot tub the following morning. That's when he rigs the camera and records the video. Of course, his face is blacked out, but it's enough to give the wives grief."

By now, I was halfway through my martini. "Wow, what a creep," I blurted out. "I'd do anything to bag this guy."

"Really, anything?" he asked. The look on his face was priceless.

"Let me clarify," I responded. "I'll do whatever it takes to satisfy your clients and get this asshole off their case. I do, however, draw the line at nudity, so don't expect me to get naked with this twerp. A little spit swapping I might be able to manage." By this point, I was struggling to enunciate. The alcohol was definitely taking its toll. "Will that be enough?"

"Diana Darling, that would be perfect. We just have a couple more things to plan," James said.

"Go for it," I said. His right cheek was doing that tweaking thing again. I wanted to ask why he kept using my first and last name. Perhaps it was just his style, and in all honesty, at this point I couldn't care less.

"Now about that dress you hung up in the closet. It's lovely, but not exactly what I had in mind for you for tomorrow's dinner event," James said.

"Okay, so you have something better?" Already he'd promised the Jimmy Choos; now it appeared I might be adding to the list. This just kept getting better and better.

"I saw a little black number at the ladies fashion store, when I checked out the shoes. A Paris label. You're about a size ten, right?"

By now, I was munching on my second gin-soaked olive. "You're right on, Jimmie." He winced when I said that. It was time to press forward. "Oh, and while you're there, it looks like I'll be requiring a bathing suit for the hot tub."

"I presume you're a one-piece swimsuit kind of girl?"

"Ya got that right."

"Change of plans. It's going to be a bikini," he said with a grin.

One the thing I was grateful for was keeping in shape. I ran, biked, and swam three times a week, all for free. I reckoned I could pull off wearing a bikini, even at my age. Besides, Andrew didn't seem to be too choosey. He was just looking for women with rich husbands. I munched on the last gin-soaked olive from my drained martini glass and said, "Well in that case, there'd better be a Hermès bag to match the dress."

James raised his glass and gently touched it against mine. He nodded as our eyes locked. The game was on.

5

I Spy theme song,
EARLE HAGEN

I wasn't used to sleeping in a king-size bed—plenty of room to sprawl and stretch. It was wonderful, and I luxuriated in the expanse, rolled under the duvet, and relished the feel of high-quality cotton bed linens. I wondered if I could slip the sheets into my suitcase before we checked out. Most times, people steal towels from hotels. Perhaps sheets would go unnoticed. Mental note to self: take the sheets, if the opportunity arises. The sheets would easily wrap three times around my single bed; I could just reposition them weekly to have a clean surface and cut down on laundry costs.

Perhaps it was the sunlight starting to spill through the partially open blinds that woke me. Most likely, it was the sound of snoring. I peered through a strategically half-open eyelid. James was no longer on the couch. He lay sprawled on the floor beside the coffee table. I really couldn't blame him. A six-foot frame won't fit on a five-foot couch. Did I feel guilty that he was now on the floor? Not on your life. Well, in all honesty, perhaps a tad guilty. But given that it was plush carpeting, he seemed to be comfortable enough.

I admired his lean torso, fantasized about his rippling abs underneath the tight T-shirt, and took in the athletic muscles of his legs, one of which was bent upright at the knee. Definitely James Woods was a fine specimen of masculinity. It also appeared he was a boxer kind of guy versus tighty-whities. Mmm, more room for . . . my mind was getting carried away. A few years of celibacy will do that to a woman in her sexual prime.

"So, Diana," he drawled, with that same fake Texan accent he manufactured at last night's session, "ya done looking?"

His eyes were still closed, so how in hell did he know I was staring? This guy must have eyeballs in places I'd never even considered. "Sorry, just didn't want to wake you up. Sleep well?" I asked, silently congratulating myself for not stuttering while I spoke.

"I've slept in worse places. So not bad, all things considered," James replied.

Did I want to know more? You bet, but as a contracted employee, I needed to maintain professional objectivity, or at least attempt it. Damn, it was hard. "So what's our plan for the day?" I asked.

James opened his eyes and sat up. Then he grabbed his notepad off the coffee table. "Continue in the same vein and with the same demeanour as last evening. Andrew has identified you as a prospect. You're doing just fine."

My cheeks flushed and I went to the closet to grab some clothes before heading into the bathroom.

"Nice kitty pyjamas," he commented over his shoulder. "The day's itinerary can wait until you're properly dressed."

So far, James was being a perfect gentleman. It was me who needed to get back in line and get my wayward thoughts in check.

Over a light breakfast, we reviewed the agenda for the day. Oh joy, we'd start off by participating in some small group work with a few other couples and a different counsellor. I wondered if we would be working with the spouse-swapping couples who were at the bar yesterday evening. In the afternoon, we'd be convening as a larger group with Andrew.

James sipped his coffee and pointed at the final item on the day's agenda: the dinner and social get-together. "This is when he'll make his connection with you."

"So how's he going to make his move if you're with me?" I asked.

"You're getting the hang of this, Diana. Unfortunately due to my *job*, as a trader in the stock market, I'll be receiving a crucial call midway through the meal. You'll be on your own for approximately twenty minutes."

I nodded. "Okay, so he'll feel compelled to rescue me from solitary dining status. How do you want me to play it? Should I be angry or a complacent wife bowing down to her husband's more important work or just plain annoyed?"

James chewed on his inner cheek, cocked an eyebrow, and simply said, "Diana Darling, I have full confidence in you. Just be yourself and let it play out."

I wasn't sure, but I think he emphasized my last name just a little too long once again. Perhaps it should have made me feel uncomfortable. Instead it felt right. In the eyes of James Woods, it seemed I was a bona fide private investigator. I couldn't wait until dinner to prove him right.

The morning and afternoon sessions were uneventful, except for one woman who chose to confront her husband about cheating. Her confrontation didn't seem to mesh with the couples retreat philosophy, and they were removed from the event. I felt sorry for the woman, as I'd been in her shoes before. Cheating spouses are like vermin—they need to be stomped on. Such is life.

Afterwards, I was eagerly waiting for dinner and for the show to begin. In the meantime, James went shopping, and I went back to our room. When he returned, he tossed a garment bag, along with a small boutique bag with pink overflowing tissues, on the bed. He nodded at the garment bag. "Time to get dressed for dinner," he said. "The other bag is for tomorrow."

...

After unzipping the bag, I gasped. The little black Paris dress reminded me of the one Audrey Hepburn wore in *Breakfast at Tiffany's*. An off-the-shoulder, scooped bodice, and skin-tight material that would hug me like a glove. My only problem was not packing a strapless bra. I've always been a creative soul, able to make do, so compared to some of the scrapes I've been in, this one was easy. Being somewhat accident-prone, I always packed a first-aid kit. My only requirement for this dress alteration was a roll of brown adhesive bandage tape. With three six-inch strips for each breast, I carefully positioned the tape from underneath with one strip on each side. Then one strip across the centre, pulling the other strips up for a snug fit. It was perfect. Would hurt like hell when I had to pull them off, but I was strapless and the girls were well-positioned.

The Jimmy Choos were a perfect fit, accenting my slender legs, even making them look longer. I carefully applied mascara and eyeliner, then outlined my lips with a lip liner and filled them in with a lip brush. After gathering my long mop of auburn hair into a loose chignon, I applied just a hint of gloss in the middle of my lower lip, pleased to see I'd achieved a pouty look. As I exited the bathroom, James seemed to be muttering something about women and bathrooms and taking too long. Then he caught sight of me.

Based on his reaction, I'd hit a home run. He was in the process of retrieving his jaw from his belly button before speaking. "Nice, very nice, Diana. You look . . ." his voice trailed off, and his hands made wavy, curvy motions in the air, "wonderful," he finally said.

I had the feeling that James wasn't often at a loss for words, so I kind of enjoyed his lack thereof. He was dressed in a tailored suit, white shirt slightly open at the collar, and he'd managed to comb his hair into something that barely resembled a crew cut. James definitely awakened a whole different side of me, even though I'd sworn off workplace relations after that Christmas party fiasco. It was time to lay low and perform the job I'd been hired to do.

James took my hand as we entered the dining room. We were one of the last couples to arrive, and I sized up the room. The spouse swappers were at a table for six; there was another table for four with an extra chair. Everyone else seemed to be at a table for two.

James leaned in close and whispered in my ear, "The hawk is at three o'clock, at the table for five. Turn and give him a smile."

I pasted on my best contrite, *poor me* smile, being lumbered with this jerk of a husband. My reward was immediate. Andrew's eyes lit up and locked with mine—a quick glance at James and then back to me. The hook and bait were set. Now all I had to do was reel him in.

Partway through the meal of overdone skewered beef, carrot medallions, and a baked potato, James reached for his cell phone. "Show time," he whispered to me.

"What do you mean?" he growled into the phone. "Can't it wait?" A few muffled expletives before he hung up and faced me.

"Really, James, couldn't you have left that damned thing in the room, at least during dinner?" My voice was just loud enough for the neighbouring diners to overhear. Sympathetic nods from the wives and envious looks from their husbands were clearly evident.

"It's work, honey. You know how important my job is. It's what affords us the lifestyle you've become accustomed to, and I know how you like your baubles and trinkets." By now, he was standing and about to exit the dining room. "I'll be as quick as I can. Probably a half hour or less."

I sighed and turned resignedly to my meal, grabbed a fork, and speared a carrot with more force than was required. In my peripheral vision, Andrew dabbed his lips with a napkin as he rose from the table and headed in my direction.

"Mrs. Woods, I couldn't help but overhear your conversation. Perhaps you'd allow me to join you until your husband returns," Andrew asked.

I nodded in assent and dabbed my eyes with a tissue. "Please, sit down," I said.

"No one should leave such an attractive woman sitting alone. If you don't mind my asking, does this happen often?"

"All the time," I replied as I injected a quiver into my voice. "It's as if he's married to his job and that damned cell phone."

Andrew's hand began to snake its way across the table, pausing briefly at the bread basket. My plate suddenly became fascinating, and I looked down, steeling myself for a response as he patted the back of my hand. I resisted the urge to reach for the hand sanitizer sample I'd put in my Hermès bag. Instead I looked him straight in the eye and replied, "You're so considerate. Thank you, Andrew."

He beamed at my response. His intentions were so obvious, it made me want to reach across the table and wrap both my hands around his scrawny chicken neck. Instead, I smiled sweetly, reminding myself I was doing this for the money, for James's clients, and for any other woman Andrew had suckered over the years. Convinced there were a large number of women, I'd do them justice.

"If you have any advice for me, I'd surely be grateful. That's why we came on this retreat in the first place. So far, I'm sorry to say it doesn't seem to be helping. James is off doing his own thing, and here I sit." My doe-eyed look seemed to give him the opportunity I was hoping for.

"Well, Mrs. Woods, I . . ." Andrew began.

"Diana, please call me Diana," I demurred.

"Diana, there is perhaps some advice I could offer you individually, but it would need to be another time. A private counselling session, if you will," Andrew said.

His eyes were intense, and he seemed really nice—totally focused on me. Had I not been aware of his history, I might even have fallen for him in another place or time.

Andrew took a quick glance at his watch before zeroing in. He had everything down to a fine art, even down to the timing. It reminded me that this was his work. I kept silent. It was time for him to make his move.

"Perhaps you'd consider meeting me tomorrow morning for a private session. We could focus on your concerns, issues, or anything you need help with," Andrew said.

"I'd do anything to save Jimmie's and my marriage. Just tell me where and when." His hesitation was palpable. It was now or never. A tear escaped my eye and trickled down my cheek. Cripes, I was getting caught up in my own acting.

James wasn't the only one who could quickly slip into role playing. I was disappointed he wasn't there to see my performance, and I was pretty sure he would have offered me some more expensive clothes. Alas, it was a solo act this time around.

"Please," I begged, after Andrew was silent for too long.

"Don't take this the wrong way, but I don't want the other women to know about this. I simply can't do this for everyone."

"I'm fine with that and besides my husband is usually doing business calls first thing in the morning."

"I'm in cabin four at the rear of the hotel. There's a hot tub on the back deck. It might help you relax, and I can take the time to listen without any other intrusions. I'll meet you there at 8:00 a.m. You do have a bathing suit, don't you?" Andrew asked.

Do I? I wondered. Oh crap, that's what was in the small bag that was still unopened in my room. "Yes, Andrew, I have a swimsuit, and thank you for inviting me."

"Diana," James said, announcing his return to the table. "Sorry to take so long. I hurried as best I could. You know the stock market. It never sleeps and is always awake in some far corner of the world."

Andrew beamed when he heard the words *stock market*. James may as well have said, *We've got money. Loads. Just come and get it.*

"Andrew, thanks for keeping the missus entertained." James turned to look at me. "And just to let you know before I forget, there's an early-morning conference call I'll need to be on. I'll make it up to you, I promise."

"Sure, Jimmie, I know you will. You always do. And Andrew, thanks for the company," I said. He patted my hand one more time for good measure, gave half a wink in my direction, and practically swaggered back to his own table. My hand immediately dove into my Hermès bag for the hand sanitizer.

"Excellent job, Diana. You had him eating out of your hand." A wide grin stretched across James's face as he bent to give me a kiss on the forehead.

I was so busy basking in the praise and the light touch of his lips that it took a moment to register. "How did you know? You weren't even here."

"Diana, one of these days I'll take you to the Spy Store. They have a slogan that says, 'In God we trust; all others we monitor.' They also have these little contraptions called *bugs*." He retrieved a tiny black transmitter from the base of the floral centrepiece in the middle of the table and stuffed it into his shirt pocket. "I was with you every step of the way."

I knew about listening and recording devices, from chapter eleven of my course, but when had they started making them so small? And where was it plugged in? My PI manual had illustrated a listening device as a chunky hidden microphone. Ah well, it was good that James had heard my performance. Just wait until tomorrow in the hot tub. That would be Oscar-worthy material.

6

Hands Up,
OTTAWAN

That night, James just skipped the couch completely, laid a blanket on the hotel room floor, and curled up. Within seconds, the soft rhythmic sound of snoring ensued. I tore the pink tissues from the small bag and pulled out a black bikini. Perhaps a bit skimpy, otherwise not too bad. Then I flipped through the TV channels and caught snippets of everything from decorating to cooking to reality shows where everyone seemed to be running out of time or money. Cheap shows to produce, I presumed, since they didn't have to pay real actors or actresses, but for whatever reason it worked.

Bottom line, I couldn't sleep, and it wasn't only about facing Andrew in the hot tub tomorrow morning. It had a lot to do with the heavy-breathing hunk of virile flesh on the floor a few feet from my bed. He awakened a different curiosity within me, mostly hormonal, and it had been a long time since I'd felt that way. Sure, I'd done a couple of test drives with men after my second divorce, and yikes, I'd rather forget them, especially the last one that left me with a bad case of poison ivy after a roll in the woods. The guy didn't even offer to pay for a two week supply of calamine lotion. What a cheapo!

After a fitful sleep, I awoke to find the little black bikini at the foot of my bed. James was already dressed and handing me a coffee. "You sure you're still okay with this?" he asked.

"Absolutely, it's about time this weasel is caught and hung out to dry." I grabbed the bikini and headed to the bathroom to change. At some point during the night, it must have shrunk because what had seemed reasonable last night when I opened the bag, today looked like a pair of postage stamp-sized nipple covers and a bottom that resembled butt floss, just with a bit more coverage in the front for the garden patch.

I cast off my kitty pyjamas and donned the required uniform for the day. The top didn't actually look too bad. Some adjustments to the straps, and I was feeling pretty good about how I looked. It was the bottom part that stymied me. It fit well enough, if you're one of those people who like having material creep up your nether regions, but it was the pruning to the front garden patch that would require attention.

Crap, I hadn't brought a razor with me, debated on having James go to the gift shop for a depilatory cream or some wax strips, but that didn't seem like a good idea. Using the tweezers in my suitcase would make me late and plucking hairs would hurt like hell, so it was time to come up with a Plan B.

James's shaving kit bag was wide open on the back of the toilet. It beckoned, so I looked. Mmm, a Schick disposable razor peaked its doubled-edged blades over the side of the bag. "You're mine," I declared. After all, I could rinse the stray hairs out, and he'd never notice the difference. At least until he tried to shave and found the blades a bit duller.

With the pruning over and no sign of bloodshed, I was ready. There was no way James was seeing me like this until absolutely necessary, so I pulled on a track suit and headed into the room.

"What, no show?" he asked.

"Later," I replied. My watch indicated five minutes to 8:00 a.m. It was time to leave. "Where will you be?"

"I've already set up along the tree line. I'll give you a ten-minute head start, just in case. Beyond that, I'll have you in my sight at all times. With the noise from the hot tub, I may have difficulty with audio. Worst case scenario, raise your left hand over your head if you're in trouble."

I tried to make light of it. "Why my left hand?"

"Because that's the one that's closest to your heart." He smiled. I didn't.

...

I closed the hotel room door and headed in the direction of cabin four. The shifting morning light cast shadows along the path that meandered towards the assigned location. Palpitations and an increased heart rate kept me company. I wasn't so nervous as much as keyed up, and that should have scared me, but it didn't. As I rounded the corner to the rear of the cabin, I saw him. Andrew was already ensconced in the hot tub, raising a glass of champagne in salute.

"Diana, I'm so glad you came. I was beginning to wonder if you had second thoughts." His voice was low, gentle, and encouraging. I felt as if I was being worked by a pro.

"No second thoughts," I replied. "Like I said last night, I'd do anything to save my marriage."

I stood on the edge of the hot tub and unzipped the top of my track suit, shivering in the cold fall day. Next I slowly slipped off my pants, taking my time to ease the elastic waistband over my hips, wiggling a bit more than was necessary. He needed to take the bait, and his appraising eyes told me I was doing just fine.

Andrew rose halfway, as if to assist me into the tub. I brushed him off and lowered myself into the swirling water. During last night's candlelight dinner, he'd looked somewhat handsome, and I understood how the other women may have been lured in. Today under the unforgiving sun, his tan looked orange and streaky—probably a spray-on product. His manscaped chest was devoid of hair, except for a few patches reminiscent of something my cat might have thrown up. He was a letch, and it was time to get on with the job I'd been hired to do.

"Oh, is that for me?" I squealed as he indicated a glass of champagne directly opposite of where he was sitting.

"I took the liberty. To help you relax a bit. Sometimes it's good to let your hair down and just be free. Go with the flow so to speak."

"Yes, Andrew, you're so right." I took a ladylike sip from the glass. In any other moment, I'd have cheerfully downed the whole flute of liquid courage and immediately asked for a refill. I was tempted to look behind me towards the tree-edged property. That had to be where James was set up, and it was comforting to know he was there.

I raised my glass, reached across to clink crystal with Andrew, and slid back to my assigned spot across from him.

"Ever think about leaving him?" Andrew questioned.

I took my time responding. The red light of a surveillance camera winked at me from the underside of the cabin's eavestrough facing the hot tub. Christ, this guy had everything down to a fine art. The set-up ensured the female face was revealed whilst only showing the back of Andrew's head.

"Oh, I couldn't ever leave him. I don't have a career, and sometimes he's a good husband. It's just that . . ."

"Just that . . . what?" he prompted.

"Sometimes, it's just so lonely." I sighed and looked down at the bubbling water.

It was time to avoid eye contact, act demure, and wait for his next move. I was definitely getting this whole waiting routine down pat. He'd have to make a move soon, as the Sunday session was scheduled to start in sixty minutes. Unfortunately for me, he seemed to be taking his time. There had to be something I could do to get him closer, otherwise I'd be sharing bathtub-temperature water with this creep for the next hour. God only knew what strain of bacteria called his body home, and whether or not the amount of chlorine bursting through the jets would be enough to kill them. I never considered myself to be a germophobe, and yet it seemed like the right time for action. My hand shook, spilling champagne into the tub. That should do it.

"Diana, you seem nervous. There's no need." He eased his way towards me across the foaming water, his clear blue eyes gleaming with delight. "Here, let me top you up." He was close now. His teeth were way too white—it reminded me of Chiclets. As I wondered what teeth whitening product he used, I stifled the urge to grab the champagne bottle out of his hand and bash him over the head with it.

His breath was hot on my cheeks as he draped an arm across my shoulder and leaned in. "You're really beautiful, you know." His voice had turned husky. Cripes, this guy didn't waste any time. Something prodded my knee. I was pretty sure it was an appendage that should have been safely tucked away inside his swimsuit. I wasn't sure how much more footage would be required for James's clients, so I held on.

"Andrew, this isn't what I was expecting. You're supposed to be here to help me," I panicked. His tiny hand slipped below the surface of the bubbling water, aimed in the direction of my right breast. I was on the verge of raising my left hand above my head when I heard a life-saving voice.

"Andrew . . . a.k.a. Dennis Moriarty, you're busted. Back off from the woman. Now!" James's voice was commanding, left no doubt as to who was in charge, and came from only a few feet behind me. Relief flooded through my body. Instincts took over. I thrust my knee into Andrew's groin with all the force I could muster. Just in case the first blow hadn't nailed the intended target, I nailed him again.

This time, I was rewarded with a groan of pain as Andrew clutched his jewels and retreated to the other side of the tub.

"You okay, Diana?" James whispered in my ear.

"Never better," I replied.

"Nice touch at the end," he said. "I wasn't expecting that."

"It was just one of those spur of the moment things. Guess I was hoping to do some damage so the bastard would be incapable of procreating." James's chuckle was all the reward I needed.

Andrew eyed us with a mixture of hate and disbelief. His head bounced like a bobblehead doll, and his eyes had turned into mere slits.

"You," he shouted. His voice was a bit higher-pitched than usual. "Both of you. Who the hell are you?"

"My name is James Woods. I'm a private detective. Unless you stop blackmailing women, we'll be your worst fucking nightmare!"

Andrew slapped his hands on the water. "So what! You don't have anything."

"Oh, but I do. I've got my own footage of this set-up including the camera over the deck eavestrough. It's the same scene you caught my clients in. The women will happily pay me for a full-page ad in the local papers, along with an anonymous posting of your activities on social media."

Andrew didn't even bother to plead innocent. He just hauled himself out of the hot tub, still clutching his gonads, and walked a tad bent over as he escaped into cabin four.

"It's okay, Andrew, James gave them a group rate," I shouted at his retreating back.

Damn, justice felt good. "So that's it? Case closed just like that?" I asked.

"Well, not quite. I'll prepare the briefs for my clients, and I'll also send a reminder to Andrew to cease and desist. He doesn't know who my clients are, so that pretty much puts a wrench into his current activities," James said.

"I was about to raise my left hand. How did you know to come?"

"Trust me, Diana. I already know how you are. If you had to swap spit with that guy, you'd have hit me up for a lifetime's worth of Listerine. Mind you, that would have been a lot cheaper than the Choos, the dress, the bathing suit, and don't even get me started on the Hermès bag."

His right cheek muscle was doing that tweaking thing again. As I stood up, steam from the tub rose with my body. I'd like to think he was eyeing me in the black bikini—hoping he would notice me. Alas, he already switched into business mode.

"Let's get you covered up. It's cold." James handed me a robe from his bag. "Put it on," he said. "We need to go back and pack our stuff."

He was already grabbing my track suit and heading down the path. Bringing the robe was a nice touch. Maybe he did care, even if it was just a little. While he checked out of the hotel, I'd still have time to cram those bed sheets into my suitcase.

The case seemed closed. At least for now.

7

Wishin' and Hopin',
DUSTY SPRINGFIELD

It had been exactly five days and eight hours since James dropped me off at the Diana Darling Private Investigator Agency. There were promises to be in touch for future cases, and he thanked me for a job well done. His cheque for two thousand dollars sailed effortlessly into my bank account, and it gave me a nice cushion from which to pay my rent and utilities. I had to admit that taking down a bad guy felt amazing. Now everything else seemed anticlimactic, so I focused on trying to develop my own list of clients.

The first day back I celebrated by buying myself a spy camera pen from the Spy Store, splurging on a cat tree for Xena, and ordering pizza.

The second day back, I wrapped the bed sheets, acquired from the hotel room, around my bed in the supply room—my sleeping quarters. The room was big enough to hold a single bed, a side table, a light, and a teeny TV. What else did one need for a bedroom? It wasn't like I was doing a lot of entertaining there, given my single status. The big plus was hiring a plumber to install a shower head in the janitor's closet. There was already taps and a floor drain, so no biggie. I got myself a flexible rod and a shower curtain liner from the Dollar Store. Life was good.

The third day back, I actually had a new case! I spent the evening freezing my butt off in a hockey arena while the coach berated one of the kids. The kid's parent, my client, wanted a witness to the alleged verbal abuse, so I got to use my new pen.

The pen was a work of art, aside from being a bit bulky, and I wasn't sure about the English translation of the Chinese instructions for using the pen. The instructions sounded a bit sketchy; I was still trying to figure out what 'in closes down and under the readiness for action, presses the button,' meant. I charged the pen from my computer and knew how to turn it off and on. It wrote like a real pen, had a camera peephole near the top for pictures or short videos, and had a microphone just under the lapel holder.

Notes were also a necessity for this case, in the event my new gadget didn't work, so I carefully took details on a pad of paper. I made sure the quotation marks were correctly placed, and damn, my grammar teacher would have been proud of me. The spelling was a bit dicey though. The coach called the kid a "stupid little fuckhead," and I wasn't sure if that was one word or two. Likewise, when the coach said, "You royally screwed the pooch!" Was that "pooch" or "pouch," and what the hell did it mean? Anyway, since the coach couldn't complete a sentence without dropping the F-bomb on some poor kid, I was pretty sure I left the arena with enough evidence to satisfy my client.

Business was picking up, and I made sure the hockey parent had a lot of my self-designed, self-printed business cards. On my card, there was a huge magnifying glass in the top right corner, with a female figure stooped as if studying something on the ground. I found the image after playing a Nancy Drew computer game, and it seemed appropriate.

On day four, I tried again to get in touch with my first client, Isadora. She hadn't answered my e-mail, so I wondered what was up. At least she'd offered to pay half of the fee up front. Perhaps the postal service was a bit slow since I was still waiting for the cheque. I sent the pictures of Baldy and Blondie to her almost a week ago. There was a niggling fear in my belly that was hard to ignore. What if Isadora didn't plan to pay the rest? I'd learned to rely on my gut instinct, and right now it was churning big time. Something was amiss, yet I couldn't quite put my finger on it. Perhaps some Chinese takeout would settle my stomach.

After an order of Kung Pao chicken with extra spicy sauce, I crawled into the supply room to watch black and white reruns of *Perry Mason* and wished I had Della Street for a secretary. That Drake guy would have to take a back seat, because I was a real PI. Mind you, he looked kind of sophisticated, and his hair was decent. It made me wonder what Andrew was up to now. Hopefully he'd gone to ground, was still limping from a groin injury, and never to be seen again.

By day five, I was restless, pacing, debated on calling James, held the phone in my hand umpteen times, but wimped out on dialling the number. One last time, and I'd go for it. But the phone rang just as I was about to pick up the receiver. Deep breath, pinch the nose, sound like a receptionist, put the caller on hold, then pretend to transfer the call to myself.

"Diana Darling Private Investigator Agency, how may I help you?" My nasal intonation was perfect.

"Diana, I know it's you."

I recognized the voice immediately. It was James. He sounded strange, not his usual composed self. My earlier belly niggles launched into action.

Before I could say a word, he interrupted, "Lock your door. I'll be there in five minutes. Can't explain right now. Just do it."

After he hung up, the empty drone of the phone was all I heard. I locked the door, closed the Venetian storefront blinds, and waited. Whatever was going on sounded serious.

A few minutes later, there was a screech of brakes, followed by pounding on the door. I cautiously peered through a window slat.

James stood on the doorstep, looking like death warmed over. Suitcase-sized bags under his eyes, with red spider webs across the whites. He stumbled through the door when I opened it. At first, I wondered if he'd been drinking. But I couldn't detect an odour of alcohol.

"I'm sorry. I may have put you in harm's way. It could be from the first case at the Whispering Pines motel, or it might be something different. Have you heard from your client? Anything from Andrew?" he inquired.

James seemed oblivious. His words were rushed, forced, and I couldn't ignore the concern in his eyes. He looked and sounded exhausted. His muscular body slumped into my office chair. "I can't stay. Think I'm being followed. Lost the tail about six blocks back. I can't let anyone find my Jeep outside your office. Don't want to lead the person to you."

My mind was racing. Already I knew something was off about the first case when I couldn't contact my client. Now here was James, looking like something the cat dragged in. He probably hadn't slept in the last forty-eight hours. And who in hell was the *anyone* or *person* he was referring to.

He tossed a cell phone on my desk. "It's a burner. I'm using one too, and my number is programmed in yours under the name Woody. We can stay in touch that way. I'll fill you in later. Gotta go," James said. Then he rose from the chair, his knees buckled, and he collapsed to the floor.

Holy shit! Should I be calling 911? His colour looked okay, and he was still breathing. "God, James, are you alright?"

"Yeah, yeah, just lack of sleep. Can't remember when I last got some shut eye."

It was time for me to take charge.

"Gimme your keys," I said. "You're not in any shape to be going anywhere." When he didn't offer the keys, I snatched them from his hand. "When you manage to scrape yourself off the floor, there's a bed in the back. I'll move the Jeep, hide it from *anyone*, and then you've got some major explaining to do."

He was getting to his feet, but I was already out the door, staring at the key fob. It was one of those electronic devices. Would it work if I just stuck the key in the driver's side door lock? There was a little button that resembled an unlock sign, so with crossed fingers, I pressed it. Rewarded with a clinking noise, I hauled ass into the seat and jammed the key into the ignition and turned it.

Nothing happened. Crap, why hadn't I noticed before that he drove a standard? A *clutch* is a term used to refer to a type of purse, not something that should be found beside a brake pedal. Okay, so maybe I had to depress the clutch first. This time the engine fired up. Now what? Oh yeah, release the parking brake. The brake creaked as I put it into a horizontal position.

My brain was scrambled. What the hell was going on with James, and why was I trying to hide his vehicle? Was my life really in danger, or was it just my overactive imagination? My last attempt at driving a standard had nearly landed me in the emergency room with whiplash, but I knew I needed to do this. Damn, I couldn't reverse. Was I supposed to pull on the rubber flange on the gearshift? Screw it, there was a slight incline in front of my office, so I put the car in neutral and coasted out of the spot. Grounded the gearshift into first, stalled it a couple of times, and lurched out of the lot.

Just a few more blocks, then I'd have my destination. As I drove, my late mother's voice resonated in my head. It was one of her favourite mantras: "If it has tires or testicles, it's going to cause you problems." And here I was with both.

"Touché! Love ya, Mom," I whispered. I might have waved a hand through the sunroof to acknowledge her, but my left was clenched on the steering wheel, and my right had a death grip on the gearshift.

The library parking lot was full of vehicles and not just for patrons. Everyone in the area used it as free parking, and it was the perfect place to hide a car. The Jeep stalled in a spot and I took it as a sign, relieved to be exiting the big black beast. The fact that it straddled two parking spaces and was on an angle didn't matter.

I half ran, half jogged back to my office while I tried to collect my thoughts. What was a burner phone? But if it was free, who cares. What did James mean when he said, "It could be something different." I unlocked the door and threw it open. It seemed empty. No one was there. Next I raced to the back where I had a two-seater couch, a mini fridge, and a microwave behind a door labelled *Photocopy Room*. The place was deserted. Had James already left?

The door to the supply room was slightly ajar. I entered. There was James curled up on my single bed, snoring his head off. To make matters worse, Xena was resting in the crook of his arm. The little shithead had betrayed me, and her eyes carried a look as if to say, *Do Not Disturb*. I closed the door, reckoning that if I used a really good brush to remove all the hair, the cat tree could be returned to the pet store. Or maybe, I'd just cut down on her treat consumption for a few days.

After the morning I had, caffeine wasn't going to cut it for me. It was only 11:00 a.m., but I hauled a box of wine out of the under-counter fridge in the photocopy room, poured a generous portion into a water glass, and slugged it back. There had to be a connection to the first case. I pulled my notes from the file drawer and reread. It seemed straightforward. I knew James had been hired by Blondie's husband, but I didn't know anything about him. My client's husband was a minister and had no money, so where was the link? What if it was Andrew retaliating for James having put an end to his lucrative business venture at the couples retreat? This was like trying to solve one of those impossible puzzles in the back of the women's weekly magazine, found near the checkout at every major grocery chain. Usually I was pretty good at the puzzles. This time, however, I was totally stymied.

Perhaps too many years of working for the government revenue agency made me suspicious. It was always about the money. Who had it? Who hid it? Where did it come from, and who paid whom? Follow the money. It was a cliché, yet one that rarely deviated from true facts. If Blondie's husband hired James, then he obviously had money. My client had a lot of money, so it seemed worthwhile to check further. I still had a few connections from my last job as an accountant, but that would be a last resort. I'd be using my new finely honed detective skills.

The effects of the wine were making me a tad lightheaded, and when the phone rang, I almost forgot to pinch my nose before answering and delivering the welcome message.

"I need to speak with Diana Darling," the caller said.

"One moment and I'll transfer you. May I tell her who is calling?"

"My name is Nikki."

"One moment please, I'll see if Ms. Darling is available."

With the caller on hold, I waited ten seconds before answering. "It's Diana." Oh crap, forgot to unpinch my nose. Perhaps she wouldn't notice.

"I found your business card at my husband's office. His name is Jimmie, and now he's missing. Something is really wrong."

Her speech was too fast, pressured, and her sentences ran together. She bordered on hysteria.

"And there's more. I think my husband is having an affair," she said.

The caller sounded a bit loopy. Think fast. "Let me take down your information. What is your name?"

"It's Nikki," she shouted. "Are you the one that's sleeping with him? Why does he have your phone number on his desk?"

This call was getting stranger by the minute. But giving up on a potential client was not an option for me.

"I have an opening at 2:00 p.m.," I said. "Perhaps we can discuss things further. Do you need the address?"

The phone slammed down on her end, and I wasn't sure if that meant a *yes* or a *no*.

It might not have been one of the smartest decisions I ever made, but given the scenario, what the hell. If I listened to James, there was reason to believe my safety may be compromised. I hid a black Jeep in a library parking lot, I was drinking wine in the morning, James was in bed with my cat, and a new client was showing up in a few hours.

It was shaping up to be a really interesting day!

8

That Darn Cat!,
BOBBY DARIN

After one more glass of wine and a couple hours of listening to the sound of contented snoring emanating from the supply room, I made a critical decision. It was time to awake the sleeping giant. My approach needed to be subtle, so I debated knocking over the garbage bin in the hallway just outside the door to create a little noise. By the time I kicked the bin three times, it was obviously not working. James was still sleeping, the metal bin had a dent in it the size of a football, Xena was still cuddled up beside him, and my foot was swollen and throbbing! So much for subtle; it was time to be more creative.

From the silverware drawer, I pulled out a packet of cat treats, careful to not make a sound. If Xena heard the wrinkle of the foil bag, she'd be here in a shot. With six treats in hand, I cautiously peeked through the partially open door to my pseudo bedroom.

James was sprawled on his back on my single bed, a contented expression on his face. Xena sat guard beside his head, posed like an Egyptian goddess and preened herself as if she just found a new best friend. Even gave me her best *stink eye* for being interrupted before going back to paw licking.

I threw the treats on James, hoping one would land in a strategic spot, and quietly closed the door. Within seconds, I was rewarded with a loud, "What the fuck." The sound of blankets being strewn, more swearing, and feet hitting the floor were like music to my ears.

I raced to the front of the office, sat in the desk chair, pretended to peruse some mostly empty files, and put on my very best innocent facial expression.

James stumbled down the hallway. "Sorry, Diana. So sorry. Guess I needed the sleep more than I thought. Not sure what the hell woke me up though."

He rubbed his eyes and reminded me of a kid who'd been awakened from a night terror. "Here, have a seat, and I'll get you a coffee. Black right?" I asked.

"Yeah," he said. Already his eyes were looking through the front door for his Jeep.

"Don't worry. It's safe, only a few blocks away." I tossed the keys to him, but couldn't resist adding, "Before I give you the location, you need to let me in on what's going on here. Have caffeine first, but I have a client coming in an hour. Will that give you enough time?"

James nodded.

I returned with two mugs and took a seat across from him. James took a slug of steaming coffee and eyed me warily.

"Okay," he finally said, running his hands across his thick brush cut. "At first I thought it was the initial case. The one where I first met you. I'd never actually met my client; it was just a phone call, and that's not common in my practice. Then I began to wonder if it was Andrew. My receptionist had her tires slashed last night and the office was broken into."

"Holy shit!" I said. "Does that happen often?"

"Not usually. And now that I've had some time to think about it, I believe it's something totally different after all." He reached for the burner phone on my desk and started playing with it.

"Not so fast. You're not getting off that easy." I extracted the free/prepaid phone from his hand and placed it in my pocket. "I deserve more of an explanation. Don't you think?"

"Yeah, yeah. You're right. Have you heard from your first client?" James asked.

"No, I haven't. But don't try and change the subject." His face took on an awkward, self-conscious expression. It appeared as if James wasn't one who often shared his thoughts, personal or otherwise. I waited, this time managing to keep silent until he spoke again.

"I have an ex-wife," his voice hesitated. "And she has some . . . issues."

"Issues, as in what kind?" I asked. This was progress. Already I knew he was single and wasn't the totally well-put-together, confident guy he pretended to be. Now this was something I could work with.

"Well, she has some mental health problems. If she stays on her medication, she's usually okay. When she goes off them, she gets delusional. Thinks I'm out to get her and can be a bit of a headcase."

"I don't get it. What's that got to do with me?" I asked.

"We're divorced, but when she stops taking her meds, she seems to forget that fact. Thinks we're still married. And if she finds me with you, she'll think I'm having an affair. That's just how her brain seems to be wired."

Fascinating, I thought. I only spent two nights with him, nothing had been consummated, and already we were a couple in someone else's eyes. "Mmm, so what happens next?" I asked.

"I'll track her down. Given her behaviour, the psychiatrist will admit her to a mental hospital for assessment, devise a treatment plan, get her back on her meds, and then she'll be okay again for a while."

I was about to ask how a smart guy like him had ended up with a crazy lady, then reminded myself I also had a couple of skeletons in my closet. Two ex-husbands in fact, and neither of them had turned out to be award winners in the spousal department. The first one liked other women. Thought I was too independent and didn't fulfill his *need to be needed*. And the second was incapable of holding down a job. Couldn't even fill out his damned unemployment forms correctly. I could empathize with James. It seemed we had a lot in common when it came to making bad relationship decisions.

"How on earth would your ex-wife know about me?" I asked. There had to be more he wasn't telling.

"When my office was broken into, the brochures from last weekend's retreat were moved on my desk. Your name and contact info were inside one of the brochures," he said.

"So tell me, James. Just how worried should I be?" He had the grace to look a bit sheepish, but I was already thinking ahead. If all of this WAS her doing, and she planned to slash my tires too, James would be paying for a brand new set of radials—expensive ones.

"I'm the one she wants. But you will need to be extra cautious until she's apprehended. I don't expect it to take much more than a day."

"What's her name, just so I know in case she tries to contact me?"

"Her name is Nikki."

Holy crap! My earlier phone call now made sense. I checked my watch, and it was ten minutes to 2:00 p.m. James was starting to get up from his chair. "I think you'd better sit down again," I said.

"Why?"

"'Cause if you stay put, it won't take a day to find her. She'll be here in a few minutes."

"Huh?" he sounded dazed, looking at me as if I was the crazy one.

"Nikki is my two o' clock appointment."

"Whoa, in that case I'll definitely be staying. For the most part, she's harmless. Just a little misguided." He raised his now empty coffee mug. "Just tell me where I can get a refill?"

"Behind the door marked *Photocopy Room*."

"Should have known." His cheek was doing that tweaking thing again.

Xena pompously followed him down the hall with nary an acknowledging look over her shoulder at me. "And you'll be getting a finder's fee bill in the mail," I couldn't resist adding as they both retreated. If I wasn't so anxious about my upcoming appointment, I'd be dismantling the cat tree and searching for the original box it came in.

Instead I smoothed the creases from my pants, tucked in my blouse, and waited. Seconds later, a car pulled up beside my Hyundai. Nikki looked innocent enough—a petite blonde dressed in designer clothing, from her Yves Saint Laurent jacket and matching mini leather skirt to her, yup, Jimmy Choo high-heeled shoes. Now I knew where James got his fashion information from.

I took note—no knife in her hand to slash my tires. Darn, no new rubber this time around.

Nikki breezed through the door and promptly sat in the chair James had just vacated.

"I have an appointment with Ms. Darling," she gushed.

"That would be me." I raised a hand to shake hers. She ignored me.

"Oh," her voice shifted, taking on a challenging tone. "I thought you were just the receptionist. You're not what I was expecting. Jimmie usually has better taste."

I wasn't sure how to respond, so decided to play it safe. "So you're here about a cheating spouse? I have lots of experience with cases like yours. Let's start with some details."

Where in hell was James? I was wondering in the back of my mind. *And what would happen when Nikki saw him?* Hopefully it would be a peaceful encounter, yet one never knew with domestic disputes. They could easily flip out of control, and I was no stranger to that, since my second ex-husband's antics had ended up with a call to 911.

Her pert little nose sniffed the air like a dog following a scent. "He's here, isn't he? I smell his aftershave. Old Spice was always his favourite."

"I'm not sure what you mean. Who's here?"

"Jimmie's here." She reached into her purse and withdrew a packet of cigarettes, tapping them on the desk until one fell out. I was about to advise her there was a no smoking policy until she retrieved the next item. Fight or flight became a no-brainer. Since there was no place to run, and I didn't want to fight her, given the object in her hand, I chose *hide*.

I shoved back my chair, dropped to the floor, banged my head on the edge of the desk, and hid underneath. "GUN!" I screamed.

There was a clicking sound from somewhere over my head. Shit! It had to be the pistol's hammer being drawn back. My heart thundered in my chest. Could a bullet go through a wooden desk? I plugged my ears and waited for the blast. Holding my breath was making me feel faint. At least if I passed out, I wouldn't feel the bullet rip into me. Or would I? From my position under the desk, I saw James, from the knees down, striding confidently out of the photocopy room. Damn, he was going to get shot! I was about to shout a second warning, when . . .

"Jesus, Nikki, you know smoking's not allowed in here," James said.

A thin trail of cigarette smoke wafted down and irritated my nostrils. What was I missing here?

"You can come out, Diana. It was just a cigarette lighter shaped like a gun."

As I tried to extricate myself from the cramped space, I once more hit my head hard against the edge of the desk. Great, now I'd have matching goose eggs.

"Some jumpy little floozy you've got yourself matched up with this time, Jimmie." Nikki's voice was condescending, and I desperately wanted to take a swing at her. But if she was as sick as James claimed she was, it wouldn't be fair. I plopped into my desk chair, felt the bumps on my head, and checked my fingers—at least there didn't seem to be any blood. The room spun, and I felt as if I was strapped to a ceiling fan on low speed. Or maybe it was just the swivel chair.

"Nikki, Nikki, Nikki. You've gone off your pills again, haven't you?" James's voice was calm, yet I detected a note of frustration. Having a crazy ex-wife couldn't be easy for him. No wonder he didn't want me calling him Jimmie at the Seasons Inn. It must have dragged up some unpleasant memories.

Now what? Would she leave peacefully or have to be dragged out, kicking and screaming, from my office? Somehow the latter seemed more probable.

James reached out his left hand as if to touch the bump on the top of my head. Nikki shrieked and hurled her body across the desk. Both hands flailed in front of my face, and all I could see were her manicured nails, long like talons. She was so close I could even see the little daisies painted on her thumbs.

"Jimmie, don't you dare even think about touching that witch! I'm your wife! Not her!" Nikki yelled.

I threw myself back in my chair in an attempt to escape major damage to my face. My heels dug in, and the chair ended up ramming my bookshelf. The heavy PI course manual fell on my head, and I threw it towards the garbage can—probably where it should have been in the first place. The whole situation was over in seconds. James snapped a pair of handcuffs around both her wrists, and she was quickly detained. Nikki howled like a wounded animal as he half dragged, half carried her from my office.

"Get some ice on your head and pack an overnight bag," he said over his shoulder.

Why an overnight bag? I wondered. "Do we have another case?" I asked.

"Not yet, but I don't think your cat will know if you have a concussion. You'll be staying at my place tonight." He left with Nikki in tow.

"You're sleeping with that bitch!" The screams of his ex-wife filtered through the open door. The door had barely closed before he was back.

Nikki was handcuffed to the passenger side mirror of my Hyundai. The way she was wrestling with it made me hope it was firmly attached.

"It looks like I'll have to use your car, since mine seems to be missing," James said.

"It's not missing, James. It's safely hidden." I cocked an eyebrow at him, tossed him my keys, and was rewarded with a tweak of his cheek. Wow, it had only been a few days since I met him, and already we had our own brand of communication.

He handed me an address and said, "Meet me there. Oh, and make sure you call a cab. You shouldn't be driving." The twenty dollar bill he tossed on my desk made up my mind. More cash in the bank, and *yes* I'd be driving.

Once again, I hauled my mauve floral Wally Mart suitcase from the closet and packed my tooth brush along with a fresh pair of kitty pyjamas. My suitcase hadn't seen this much activity in the last three years. At least the suitcase was getting a lot of action, even if I wasn't.

9

Help Me Make It Through the Night,
WILLIE NELSON

I managed to retrieve the Jeep from the library parking lot. Tried to balance an ice pack on my head, but when I hit the second gear, the ice pack slid off and onto the dashboard—it was probably safer there since both of my hands were occupied. Finally I found the address. It was an upscale condominium building on Front Street overlooking the lake. Definitely not the kind of place I was accustomed to. Security at the front desk and an elevator ride later, I arrived at his suite.

The view from the tenth floor was spectacular. Only a few boats dotted the harbour. Most had been dry-docked and shrink-wrapped for the winter. The sun was starting to drift below the horizon, and the setting would have been ideal if my head hadn't felt like the size of a watermelon.

I sat at the kitchen bar in James's open concept condo, clutching a bag of frozen peas to my head. The bumps were receding, but the throbbing in my head felt like a pair of drumsticks were playing paradiddles inside.

"Any trouble dropping her off?" I asked.

"No, I called the psychiatrist once I got her in the car, so they were ready for her. She went willingly enough, once she knew there was no other way out. If you're a threat to yourself or someone else, it's an automatic 72-hour assessment period." He paused, then added,. "My legs hurt though."

"Huh? It's not like you had to run after her," I said.

"No, it's just that I didn't reposition the seat in your car before climbing in. My knees were up to my neck. Even after I shifted the seat to the far back position, it was still pretty cramped, and now I have pains in my legs. Just how short are you anyways?"

"You're the detective, James. I'm sure you'll figure it out."

The image of him crammed into my driver's seat had me grinning big time. Made me wonder what other positions he would be capable of. In spite of the pain in my head, I had a lot of questions, and now seemed as good a time as any to start asking. Besides, if I slipped up, I could blame it on a pseudo concussion.

Then, my stomach chose that moment to unleash an involuntary unladylike growl. Perhaps it was the result of skipping lunch and drinking wine in the morning. Maybe he wouldn't notice.

"You sound hungry. I can fix that."

Obviously James didn't miss much. Within seconds, he was opening the mammoth stainless steel fridge, complete with a water dispenser and ice maker. Hell, I could have fit ten of my mini fridges inside of it. Minutes later, I was dining on toasted poppy seed bagels, slathered with cream cheese, topped with smoked salmon, and garnished with a sprinkling of capers and a dash of lemon juice. It was like an orgasm in my mouth.

"God, you're good, James."

"I know," he smiled.

His gaze was intense, and I was totally flustered. In my head, I wanted to do a tumble in bed with him, no holds barred—just a one-off get it on. But I knew that wouldn't work. It would complicate things, and it was time to return to safer ground. Redirect the conversation to work. "So have you heard from your client; the one who hired you for that case at the Whispering Pines motel?"

"No, I haven't. And to be honest, there's something really off about that whole scenario."

"How so?"

His response was lost on me. As I tried to stand up from the bar stool, I was consumed by a wave of dizziness. The room was spinning, the floor was tilting, and I grabbed the countertop for support. Strong, solid arms immediately wrapped around me. His touch made me feel even more lightheaded. Vibrations in a part of my anatomy that I thought healed over from a lack of use had resonated to life, like a flower about to bloom.

"Hey, girl, take it easy." His voice was husky and so close. His warm breath caressed my cheek. I closed my eyes, determined to hang onto this moment for as long as I could.

James scooped me up and gently set me down on a leather sofa, carefully positioned a pillow under my head, and covered me with a blanket.

"You need to sleep for a couple of hours. I'll wake you, check for any symptoms of a concussion, and then we'll go from there. By then, I'll have a plan," James said.

His words sounded repetitive, like an echo coming from a distance, and I was feeling woozy. My nether region still thrummed. Before drifting off, I made one critical decision. If I had the chance to spend any more overnights with him, I needed to be more appropriately dressed. The damned kitty pyjamas would be going to Goodwill. It was time for something completely different! Maybe even racy, or maybe nothing at all!

...

I wasn't quite sure how I found myself in his bed. The digital alarm clock read 4:00 a.m. The throbbing in my head was just a minor annoyance now. I was acutely aware of being under the sheets and that he was sleeping on top of a comforter beside me. I felt around beneath the sheets. Okay, so I was still in my clothes. James's arm was wrapped around me as I lay on my side. We were like two spoons in a cutlery drawer, and if I had a concussion, it would just have to wait. James had had less sleep than me over the past couple of days, and the last thing I wanted to do was disrupt this blissful feeling of snuggling up to a really hot guy.

I must have drifted off again because when I opened my eyes, his side of the bed was empty. His pillow was cool to the touch. He'd been up for a while. The aroma of freshly brewed coffee led me to the kitchen. Sunlight beamed through the floor-to-ceiling windows as James placed two mugs of java on the counter. His tight white T-shirt left nothing to the imagination. His baggy track pants hid plenty, or so I fantasized.

"Sleep well?" he asked.

"I could ask you the same thing. Weren't you supposed to be waking me up to make sure I didn't have a concussion?" I asked. Who was I kidding? Since James had picked up on my tummy rumblings from the night before, I was pretty sure he wouldn't miss anything serious like a brain injury.

He simply smiled. "I did wake you up, not once but twice. Both times you told me to *fuck off*. I presumed you were fine."

There was no good answer for that. It was time to move on to business. "So do we have another case or not?"

"Diana, one of the things I really like about you is your focus. You're always on the job. Yes, we have a case. For the life of me, I can't get past that whole Whispering Pines deal. Something is really off here, and I don't like to be taken advantage of. I think we're being set up. I've got some preliminary info. You okay to follow through with me?"

A thousand questions assaulted my brain. Not sure what I was getting myself into. But if James was along for the ride, I was definitely in!

"Absolutely," I replied.

"So let's start with presuming everyone is a suspect, and we'll gather background information on all of them."

I took a sip of coffee, noticed he'd already added the required cream, and nodded in assent. "So who's first on the hit list?"

"We'll start with the blonde woman and move on to the so-called minister. Next we'll take a look at your client, Isadora, and my client, Nigel. This is turning out to be more complicated than I'd originally thought."

Since it was his plan, and he had a ton of more experience than I did, it sounded great. He handed me an address on a piece of paper. "The blonde woman's a waitress. Has an evening shift here tonight. Meet me there at 10:00 p.m.," James said.

"No problem. So we'll be on a fact-finding mission."

"You got it. Now, we can't look like we know each other. I'll go in first and grab a table around 9:00 p.m. An hour later, you'll arrive and take a seat at the bar. Try and make a connection with her. I'll do the same, just from a different angle. Otherwise, we'll let it play out and compare notes afterwards," James said.

"So, James, are you going to try and pick me up?" I couldn't resist asking.

"Nah, I already did that last night when I carried you from the couch to the bed."

I winced. To divert the conversation, I tossed the keys to his Jeep on the counter and lied, "A friend drove me here."

He smiled, and I tried to ignore his all-knowing glance. Then, I looked at the paper on the counter and read the address. Holy crap! "James, you know this is a strip club, don't you?"

James R. Woods simply eyed my *slept-in* wrinkled pyjamas and sighed. "Yup! Can't wait to see what you're going to wear!"

10

The Stripper,
DAVID ROSE

I closed my eyes, rifled through the pages of the dictionary, and selected a spot about a third of the way through the book. The word I landed on would be my word for the day—a habit I learned from my mother. "Pick a word, any word, and find uses for it. It helps expand your vocabulary," she'd always said. Part of me wished I remembered to do this on a daily basis. Today seemed like a good day to test it out. I mean, she'd been right about the tires and testicles thing, so clearly she was a smart woman.

The word I landed on was *incongruous,* meaning things that don't fit together. Like hiking boots with an evening gown, an anorexic sumo wrestler, or me wearing kitty pyjamas to attract James.

The last thing I expected was to find a use for my word of the day here. *Here* being outside a strip club.

It was a decrepit-looking building on the edge of town, with windows fully shuttered for the day or night crowd, and plain clapboard siding that cried out for a new paint job. An old Pontiac Parisienne, a rusted Cadillac, and an antiquated Winnebago were parked in the lot. Judging by the number of motorcycles also parked outside, it was clear this venue was frequented by bikers.

A vintage Harley-Davidson was parked in the handicap spot. There was even a wheelchair sticker next to the licence plate. It made me wonder how the biker had gotten into the bar; it was definitely incongruous. I wiggled my fingers at the moon in salute to my mother. She would have been proud of me for doing the word of the day thing, probably wondering what in hell I was doing at a joint like this.

Mind you, my mother was not your average parent. She was the town witch and local psychic in the small town I grew up in. No wonder I pursued mathematics and number crunching. Facts and figures were something I could relate to and kept me grounded. Mom, on the other hand, tended to be a bit of a free spirit. Another one of her favourite lines was, "If you haven't grown up by the time you're sixty, you don't have to!" Given that I'd just turned forty, I reckoned I had another twenty years to test the limits.

It was late evening, and half of the neon lights cresting the signage on the gable of the building were burnt out. All I could discern was something resembling *Th . . . Muff . . . Dive . . .* Had I not already known that it was a strip club, I may have thought it had something to do with mufflers. Or perhaps the bar was frequented by swimmers?

I'd searched my wardrobe for something appropriate to wear to the strip club. Another oxymoron Mom would enjoy. Since the patrons were most likely there to look at naked flesh than a fully clothed woman, my attire probably didn't matter. Still James would be there, so I decided on a pair of skin-tight jeans, cropped mid-calf to show off my tattooed ankle, just in case I needed to compare tats. I'm still not sure how I ended up getting inked. On my last birthday, a friend had taken me to a place called *Tip of the Needle*, after a few vodka shooters. My recollection is somewhat faint, but I do recall saying, "At my age, it has to be somewhere where it won't sag." The tattoo artist had been thrilled with his creation; he even took a picture of it with a quarter taped to my ankle to show off the intricacy of his work. When I awoke the next morning, I had a tattooed ankle bracelet with a dangling scorpion finely detailed. The afterpain had been minimal, and tonight my tattoo might provide an inroad into information.

My red low-cut T-shirt had a sequined outline of a wine glass in the centre that read, *Fight like a girl. Drink like a lady.* A short, fitted black leather jacket from Value Village completed my ensemble. I debated on the Jimmy Choos, instead I settled for a pair of low-heeled pumps, just in case I needed to run.

On the way to the strip club, I also made sure to drop in at a convenience store to pick up a pack of cigarettes. One can never underestimate the bond between a group of smokers, and I was pretty sure there'd be a few hanging around in need of inhalation/respiratory therapy. Sure enough, as I pulled into the parking lot, there was a crowd huddled outside on the patio, smoke rising in puffy clouds above their heads. I patted myself on the back for thinking ahead, and that's when I spotted the Harley in the handicap spot.

The security guard outside had his arms crossed over his muscular chest, with biceps the size of my waist, and there was just too much hair everywhere. He had a unibrow and an unkempt beard that tumbled halfway to his belt buckle. Even his ear canals sprouted hair that looked dry on the ends—kind of like Xena's cat grass when I forgot to water it.

I couldn't resist giving the Harley a caress as I approached the front door. It was midnight black, with sleek lines and a powerful-looking engine. "What a sweet ride," I said to the security guard. "Who owns it?"

"That'd be Dave. He runs this joint."

"Tell him he has good taste," I said.

"You can tell him yourself. He'll be just inside the front door, to the left. Dave likes to check out the ladies. If you're looking for a job, he's your man. You might be a real contender."

His eyes took me in from head to foot, lingered over my cleavage, stopped just below my waist for a tad too long, then gazed at the rest of my legs. "Nice bit of ink on your ankle. Reckon Dave's gonna like you!"

I bit my tongue, shuddered under his gaze, and wished I'd remembered to pack the hand sanitizer after he patted me on the shoulder. But it didn't matter. James was inside, and we were on the case. It was time to get down to business.

The security guard hauled the double doors open, and in I went.

Loud music assaulted my ears; an undulating bump and grind song from the seventies. It took me a moment to acclimate. The rear of the room was in semi-darkness, but my eyes were immediately drawn to a well-lit stage. The stripper had me aghast. She looked like she should have been collecting a pension cheque instead of trying to bend her body around a slim metal pole.

Mind you, she was pretty agile, and I was reasonably impressed. Her Dolly Parton-styled hairdo was firmly sprayed into place and didn't even budge as she gyrated on the platform. I spotted a banner above the top of the stage. Her name was Tribal Tits, and it seemed appropriate since the paste-on gold nipple tassels pointed at her feet. The silicone implants were obvious, albeit they were a bit droopy, and the left was a tad lower than the right. They kind of did a wobbly dance of their own as she shifted and wrapped her legs around the pole. It was incongruous. Wow, it was my second use for the word in less than five minutes. Mom would have been over the moon.

Based on the applause and hoots and hollers from the crowd, it seemed apparent this stripper was a favourite. I left her to do her thing and headed to the bar. Now, bars can sometimes be tricky places, especially if there are regulars. You can't sit on someone's favourite bar stool or sit in between two patrons who are having a conversation, even though there might be a vacant seat in the middle. Bar politics can be complicated, and trust me, I learned my lesson more than a few times.

Thank God there was an empty bar stool at the end of the bar, and even though my back would face the door, I hiked myself up and on. I desperately wanted to look around for James, but knew that wasn't part of the game plan. "We have to look like we don't know each other," he'd said. I could do this.

"You're new here. What can I get you?" the bartender asked. He was drop-dead hunky and definitely an improvement over the security guard.

Given the array of liquor bottles on the well-stocked shelves and the number of beer taps, I figured wine was out of the question. "How about just a draft ale," I said.

"Do you want the ladies version or a full pint?"

The bartender's eyes were dark brown, like molten chocolate, and if James hadn't been in the building, I'd have been in instant lust. After all, what woman can resist chocolate? Plus, it once again reminded me how long I'd been without any kind of sexual encounter. I struggled to put my thoughts in order.

"Let's make it a pint," I smiled.

Besides, he was a potential source of information on Blondie, and it was damned hard to take my eyes off him. He expertly tipped an empty glass under the spout of Rickard's Red and poured, leaving just the right amount of foam on the top. Too much foam and customers would complain about being ripped off. Not enough and *yikes*, they'd say there wasn't enough carbonation. This one looked perfect.

"Cheers," he said and set the drink in front of me, before leaning in. "Gotta ask though. Are you sure you're in the right place?" His voice was hypnotic and deep, with a melodic hint of someone who'd recently moved from the Caribbean. He was so close to me. His warm breath caressed my cheek.

"Yup, I'm sure." It was hell on wheels to stay focused; even had to reposition my feet on the rungs on the bar stool to stay upright.

"Well, let me know if there's anything you need. Anything at all. Oh, and by the way, my name is Teddy." There was no mistaking the innuendo. It seemed I had made an impression. As he left to serve another customer, I swivelled around on the bar stool to scope out the scene.

Chapter ten from my online private investigator course was about surveillance—looking for details or anything that could be important. The course advocated using all of your senses; maybe even that sixth sense, otherwise known as intuition. For now, I'd focus on who Blondie interacted with, what her demeanour was, if she looked upset, and if Baldy showed up here. All were clues that could be important to the case. More importantly, I wanted to see where James was sitting.

Wow, what a crowd. The place was nearly full, and not with the type of patrons I expected. It seemed the stripper wasn't the only one who looked as if they were collecting an old age pension, a.k.a. Cash for Life. Had I arrived on Seniors Night? No wonder the bartender was giving me the eye. I was the only woman in the building on the right side of sixty!

There were half a dozen canes hanging over chairs, plus a lot of men with white or thinning hair and the occasional woman. I scanned the crowd for bald-headed patrons. Alas, Baldy was nowhere to be found. But then again, a minister at a strip club would have been, you guessed it, incongruent.

I spotted James, deep in discussion with a guy just by the front door to the right, and a fold-up walker was propped against their table. He had to be talking to Dave, the owner. Great, James was already down to business, and there was Blondie carrying a loaded tray to their table. She was pretty hard to miss, stuffed into red spandex pants and a black tube top that was threatening to slip. Not sure why, but I suddenly had a mental image of her getting dressed. It was probably like trying to squeeze toothpaste back into a tube once its already been squeezed out. When James stuffed a couple of bills into her cleavage, I almost choked. Blondie gave him a toothy grin and wiggled herself back to the bar to pick up the next order.

Three trips later, she plopped herself down on an empty bar stool beside me. "Never seen you here before. You looking for a job?"

"Just drowning my sorrows. This seemed as good a place as any." I was pleased with myself for being able to think on my feet.

"Man trouble?" she asked.

I shrugged. "What else?"

"Welcome to the club." She eyed the pack of cigarettes sticking out of my jacket pocket. "I'm due for a break. Wanna join me for a smoke? It'd be nice to talk to someone without grey hair."

Who was she kidding? I could already see the skunk stripe on her roots, and in all honesty, it wasn't like Baldy had a full head of hair. "Sure," I replied. "I could do with some fresh air."

Fortunately, she hadn't spotted the spy camera pen in my jacket pocket. It had taken a few goes, but I figured out how to download the data from the pen onto my computer earlier today.

Now, the blue light was on, and I was wired for audio and video. I followed her outside to the now mostly deserted patio. I would have offered her a cigarette, but the ones I picked up were the high-filter, low-nicotine brand. She'd have to suck her brains out to get a hit, and I figured that wasn't her style. Since she had her own, it didn't matter.

We were only a couple of minutes into the smoke break when her breasts started to vibrate. "Sorry, gotta take this," she said as she pulled a cell phone from her cleavage.

I moved away to give her some privacy, stayed close enough to hear her side of the conversation, and tried to make sure my pen was facing the right direction. "Hi, sweetie, can't talk long. I'm just on a break." There was a long pause as she listened. "What the fuck?" she shouted. "What makes you think someone's onto us? We've been careful!"

Holy crap, she had to be talking to the minister. I wanted to edge closer, but forced myself to stay away. Even drew in a puff on my cancer stick and tried not to inhale.

"Tomorrow," she said. "I'll meet you at the usual place." Another pause, then "Of course I know you have work on Sunday morning. I'll meet you there. Make sure it's a good collection plate tomorrow."

Wow, I couldn't wait to tell James. Struggling to stay in character, I said, "Looks like I'm not the only with problems."

She stomped her cigarette butt out on the patio floor, gave it an extra twist with her heel, and then looked at me. "Honey, you have no idea." Then, she gave me another curious look. "That reminds me. You never really answered my question from before. Why are you here?"

Uh-oh, Blondie was sounding a tad suspicious. "A place like this is great. I can have a couple of drinks, and if I need to, I can probably outrun most of the men."

"Ya got that right," she giggled. "Seriously though, if you're looking for a job, I'd be more than happy to introduce you to Dave."

"Nah, it's okay. Thanks anyway." I tossed my cigarette on the patio, glad to be rid of it. Maybe I should have felt bad about littering, but honestly the area was already covered with old cigarette packages, paper bits, dead leaves, and all sorts of crap.

"Just a thought. The strippers do well in tips, and you've got the body for it. Anyways, gotta get back to work," she said.

For the life of me, I couldn't figure out why she was working as a waitress. According to James, her husband was loaded. It just didn't make sense. Plus, there hadn't been a course for strippers on the flyer I'd gotten through the mail. Made me wonder if you just had to dance and be able to take off your clothes to the music, or was there really a class for that?

I checked out the ladies bathroom on the way back in. Darn beer always seemed to go right through me. On the inside of the stall door, phone numbers were posted. *For a good time call Jerry. Live out your fantasies with Mike.* The last one simply said, *I'm old but I'm not dead.* I couldn't wait to get out of there. How those guys had gotten into the ladies lavatory was a mystery I didn't want to solve.

Back at the bar, I casually raised my left hand as if to stretch. It was a signal I had with James to let him know either I'd had enough or I had information as to where Baldy was. Or at least where he would be tomorrow. I couldn't wait to impress him. Thankfully, this time he wouldn't be rescuing me from Andrew in a hot tub.

The bartender was already pouring me another draft, mistaking my hand signal for a refill request. I motioned for just half of the glass. He gave me a wink, pulled the tap until it reached two-thirds full, carefully placed the glass in front of me, and leaned in close. "Like I said, anything you want."

The scent of Old Spice from behind me reminded me why I was there in the first place. James rested his arm across the back of my bar stool.

"Back off on the lady," the bartender growled. His voice had gone from melodious to down-right possessive.

"Sorry, man. Didn't know she was yours. Just want to pay my tab." James's voice sounded slurred, although I knew him well enough by now to know he could launch into role playing in a heartbeat.

"Coming up."

As the bartender left to ring up the tab, James whispered in my ear, "Got some great stuff. Meet me at the coffee shop around the corner, and we'll compare notes. Bottom line, you're going to need another wardrobe change."

"Huh?" I asked. What was he thinking? If he wanted me to get up on the stripper stage, the last thing I needed was clothes! Sometimes, James could be an enigma, and sometimes he could be just downright frustrating. I was relieved when he delivered the next sentence.

"Tomorrow is Sunday, and we'll be going to church. I'll call you in five minutes so you have an excuse to leave the bar. Do me a favour. Leave the bartender behind."

11

Ring of Fire,
JOHNNY CASH

I parked next to James's Jeep and headed into the coffee shop, brimming with news. At least the crowd here seemed normal. Mind you, it wasn't like I frequented a coffee shop at midnight. There were already some teenagers, too young to visit bars without fake IDs, probably needing a place to hang without intrusive parents looking on. A middle-aged couple stumbled through the maze of tables and mismatched chairs. I reckoned they were trying to sober up before driving. The coffee shop was next door to a bar, so whoever owned the coffee shop probably made a killing from the nearby customers. It was a prime real estate location. But it was the follicly challenged man that caught my eye. He was staring at the TV, watching the news scroll across the screen.

Holy shit! It was Baldy. The last time I saw him, he'd been naked, except for the motel towel wrapped around his waist. I ducked my head and looked for James, wondering if he'd also spotted Baldy. The good reverend obviously wasn't at home working on his sermon for the next day. And if Blondie happened to arrive later, it could be a recipe for disaster. Thankfully, I'd opted for the low-heeled pumps instead of the Choos, because if she showed up, I'd be haulin' ass out of there.

I felt a light tap on my shoulder. "Glad you decided to leave the bartender behind." James's voice held a hint of mirth as he guided me to a booth near the back. "We'll be out of sight here, for the most part, and there's a back door nearby in case we need to make a hasty exit."

Trust James to always have everything covered.

I wanted him to talk first in our debriefing session because I was sure my information would top his, but the damned beer had taken control of my tongue.

"Did you see who's here?" I blurted out.

"Yup, saw him the moment I walked in. He's been on his cell phone a couple of times, and I'm pretty sure he's not calling Isadora."

"He called Blondie when we were out having a smoke. I have it recorded on my spy camera pen. Mostly it sounded like they'd been found out or that someone was following them. She seemed pretty upset. Made a comment about hoping there was a good collection plate tomorrow and that she'd meet him at the usual place after."

"Mmm," James said, looking pensive. "So no mention about man trouble, like her husband is missing or mad at her?"

"Nope. Nothing even close to that. She wasn't even wearing a wedding band." I clearly wasn't getting his message. "What makes you think her husband is missing?"

He hesitated, "Not sure, but when I figure it out, I'll clue you in. The pieces just aren't fitting together for me. There has to be more. Otherwise, what else did you learn?"

My beer-loosened tongue babbled on, "Back to Baldy and Blondie. What if they're stealing from the church? All those well-meaning people who donate are being ripped off." My voice rose, and heads were turning to look at us.

"It's okay, sweetie. I promise I'll try better." James patted my hand and leaned across the table to give me a kiss. "You might want to try and keep it down a notch," he cautioned, after moving his lips from mine. "Don't want to create a scene."

I glanced around. Baldy seemed absorbed in the TV and the middle-aged couple staggered out the door, coffee cups in hand. That was good because if they were driving under the influence, I wanted them to have a really good head start before I had to head home. "Sorry, James. So what did you find out?" I whispered.

"You're really good at this you know. The whole cigarette thing, and sidling up to the bartender like you did; that was excellent," James said.

I felt my cheeks flush and welcomed the praise. The touch of his lips on mine still lingered. Even if it was just for show, I wasn't going to complain. The last time someone had kissed me on the lips wasn't even in my remote memory, except for that drunken boss at the Christmas party a year ago. It wasn't exactly a lip kiss, more of a throat exploration, and in retrospect, I wish I'd bitten his tongue. Hindsight is 20/20, and I wished I'd been smarter back then.

"So what did you find out?" I repeated. James was good at side-tracking me, and I wasn't about to let him go without sharing.

"Well, according to Dave, the owner of the strip club, Blondie, actually her name is Bambi, has some biker connections. If she really wanted to get rid of her spouse, they could be a great resource for her. Bikers are sometimes incongruent. What you see is not what you get. They'll do the bikers ride for kids at Christmas, as if all is good, but the seamy underbelly, like drug trafficking, prostitution, and hits are part of their culture. They're brothers, in a sense. And you don't fuck with a brother."

I was still stuck on his use of the word *incongruent*. That made three times the word has popped up in less than four hours. Mom must be rolling over in her grave by now, trying to give me two thumbs-up. Since she insisted on being cremated, the thumbs thing was definitely out of the question.

"But that doesn't explain why you think your client is missing, and as a matter of fact, so is mine. I haven't received any payments, and there's been no contact since I was hired! Maybe Bambi had her husband and Isadora killed, and that's why I haven't been paid," I said, feeling confused.

The dots weren't connecting, and I hated when that happened. In fact, it was giving me a worse headache than I had after hitting my head underneath my desk yesterday. *How long do concussions last?* I wondered. *And doesn't a person with a head injury need to be closely observed for the first 48 hours?* Maybe I could spend another night at James's condo. Perhaps this time we'd both be under the covers. My mind wandered, heading in a southerly direction. I crossed my legs, trying to ignore the warm, pleasant feeling that bloomed within. My hormones were running amuck, and I struggled to focus.

James continued, "Think about it. With Isadora out of the picture, the minister stands to inherit a lot of money. Bambi's husband is a real estate developer, and he's loaded. With both of them gone, the money's up for grabs, unless they each had a really good up-to-date will. And most people don't."

"You're right," I admitted. "There has to be a connection, but how?"

A million possibilities flew through my head. Most seemed improbable. *Back to basics*, I decided. Finally my brain synapses started firing on all cylinders. After all, I was numbers person, a good one at that, and I knew where to go with this.

"Get me whatever info you have on Nigel, and I'll do some digging into Isadora's background," I said. "Then, we can compare notes. I'll see if I can run the financials, take a look at income tax stuff, money transferring, cash withdrawals, credit card use, the whole gamut. I might need to pull in a few favours from my previous job." And in that moment, I was glad I hadn't bitten my boss's tongue.

James's smile was the only reward I needed. I was about to take a sip of coffee when a warble of sirens went off in the distance. They became louder, closer. Flashing red and white strobe lights winked through the windows of the coffee shop and flew past us. It must be serious. Sounded and looked like the police, fire, and ambulance all responding. I figured it was the intoxicated couple who had stumbled out of the coffee shop. Perhaps found in a nearby ditch. I hoped they were okay and hadn't harmed anyone else.

James barely flinched at the sound. But he'd been a cop before opening his own business. Probably immune to the sound and probably set off a few sirens himself. He sure as hell set my inner sirens off.

A chair crashed over. All of a sudden, Baldy raced out of the cafe. Maybe he'd had a moment of reflection, rethinking his sermon for tomorrow. Still, that seemed like a pretty drastic response. I couldn't imagine Noah's Ark was sinking, and he was just finding out about it now.

James grabbed my hand and pointed at the TV monitor. "Breaking news . . . fire erupting on the patio at a local strip club . . . two people injured . . . stay tuned and we'll take you live on scene . . . as soon as we get there."

I was already grabbing my jacket. "Shouldn't we be going?" I asked.

"Nah, let's just watch it from here. I still have some connections with the police. I feed them info from time to time, and they reciprocate. We're safer here."

My hands trembled. If anyone was inevitably going to be injured, I hoped for the security guard. Maybe even the guy who'd scrawled the message in the bathroom stall about *being old but not dead yet*. But please don't let it be the bartender with the chocolate eyes.

Somewhere in my brain fog, it registered. I'd thrown my still-lit cigarette on the patio. Was the fire my fault?

"So we're just going to sit here and wait?" I couldn't believe James could be so nonchalant. There was obviously a lot about him I didn't know, but since he had more experience than me, I followed his lead.

"Yes, we're going to wait. It's better to watch things from here for now," he said.

My stomach was about to let out a growl, and I clenched my fist to it, hoping to stifle the sound.

"Hmm, hungry? Bet you forgot to eat again." His cheek was doing that tweaking thing, and he was already signalling a waitress over.

One grilled cheese sandwich and some fries later, I was feeling sated. I was still curious about the fire—though that would have to wait, as the cable from the TV was sketchy. James's cell phone rang in the midst.

"Got it. Thanks for the info." He hung up, scribbled an address on the back of the receipt stub, and said, "Meet me here tomorrow. Like I said earlier, we're going to church."

12

Take Me to Church,
HOZIER

When I arrived, I double-checked the address James had given me last night. If this was a church, it sure wasn't what I was expecting. Churches were supposed to be majestic stone structures, or at least brick and mortar, with stairs leading to wooden double doors. The stairs were symbolic. Newlyweds descended the stairs amid a shower of confetti to begin a life together; returning a year later to ascend with a newborn for baptism; and much later, descending one last time in a coffin, taking those final steps up to Heaven. Or for some, if they chose a life of crime and blasphemy, it could have been a shorter commute to somewhere really hot, otherwise known as Hell.

I never even realized I had a stairs fetish till I bumped into this church that didn't have any. And really, the lack of stairs was the least of it. Obviously, it had been a long time since I'd been to church because this one definitely did not fit the profile.

First of all, it was in the middle of a shopping mall. The overhead sign read, "The Church of Faithful Followers. Seek and ye shall find." *Followers of what?* I wondered. Was this a cult? There was a religious-looking cross on the sign, along with a pentagram in a circle that looked to be pagan. A smiling Buddha decorated one side, and on the other side was a peace symbol reminiscent of the sixties. If this was a church, it sure as hell was like a Mulligan stew of beliefs. I couldn't wait to go in and see who was there, but I had to wait for James.

To kill time, I checked out the shops on either side of the so-called church. To the right was a sports bar advertising the day's soccer games and happy hour starting at noon. On the left was a lingerie boutique with an impressive display of scantily clad mannequins. I was busy eying the black butt floss on one of the plastic models, wondering how uncomfortable it would be to wear, when James arrived.

"See anything you like?" he asked.

"Nope, just doing some surveillance," I replied. Who was I kidding? If I ever got a really good case that paid well, I'd be back to do some shopping. The black strapless push-up bra was amazing and sure beat using tape to strap the girls in place, like I had to do at the couples retreat last weekend.

"Good. We've got a few minutes before we go in. I presume you checked the news this morning?" James asked.

"Sure did. Details were sketchy though. Any idea who was injured?"

"You can relax, Diana. The bartender is just fine."

I hated the twinkle in his eyes. This guy could read me like a book, and the last thing I wanted was to be predictable. If only there was online course on how to be mysterious and captivating for middle-aged women like me. But that would have to wait. I decided to take the high road and ignored his comment. "So who did get hurt?"

"Well, according to my cop friends, there were only minor injuries. Tribal Tits, the stripper, will be looking for a new hairdo. Apparently she was near the fire, and her overuse of hairspray caused her head to ignite. The other victim was the security guard who threw himself across her to put the fire out. He's got some burns to the chest and his ears."

Given the size of the security guard, Tribal Tits was lucky she wasn't in need of facial reconstruction. I wondered if her silicone implants ruptured or exploded when he threw himself across her, or perhaps he had some dents in his chest. My woolgathering would have to wait. It was time to move on.

"Any idea what caused the fire?" I held my breath, not wanting to believe it was my fault.

"Could have been anything. The fire marshal is investigating, and for now the place is closed down. Looks like it started in a pile of dead leaves by the patio."

I nodded. James didn't need to know about my lit cigarette casually tossed over the patio railing, and since the evidence had probably been burned, no use admitting to it. Besides, I was going to church. Maybe I could confess and be redeemed.

James checked his watch. "So let's not keep the good minister waiting," he said. He casually took my hand, and we strolled through the glass doors. I struggled to ignore the heat, from his palm in mine, and the connection that radiated throughout and travelled downward.

Inside the foyer was a board advertising upcoming events. Movie night with Reverend Mary, lotus tea circle, blue star meditation, Zen reflection, and Kriya yoga were all on the menu. I shook my head, again wondering what kind of church this was.

I'm not exactly the church-going type, yet I felt like a Baptist at a nudist camp. James didn't seem bothered in the least.

We settled into a couple of comfortable theatre-style chairs in the back row and watched as others entered. I kind of wondered why there weren't any pews—those hard-to-sit-on wooden benches, which were the icon of churches, that I remembered from my youth. That is until Mom decided she was pagan, and we stopped going to church. Maybe today's religion was more focused on marketing and attracting a different crowd? If it's comfortable, they will come?

In this church, it was a motley crew for sure, and the ages ranged from newborns to those about to pass over. Lots of chatter; it was obvious these people were frequent visitors. The background music was reminiscent of what you hear when you're put on hold after calling a government office or perhaps in an elevator.

I checked my watch. Only five minutes until Baldy would make an appearance. This time, I hoped he was wearing a full-length robe, preferably one that didn't have the Eager Beaver logo stitched on it. A late entrant breezed through the door and took a seat two rows in front of us. Even without the red spandex pants and black tube top, I recognized her immediately and gave James a nudge.

"Okay, saw her," he whispered.

Blondie, a.k.a. Bambi, seemed to be a frequent flyer at the church, shaking hands with other parishioners and saying hellos all round. There were approximately a hundred people in the room. Minutes later, Baldy took his place at a lectern in the front of the room. A full-size statue of Mary stood on his left, and a bust of Elvis was on his right. I was just happy to see the good reverend was fully clothed. His long, white garment touched the ground and a bejeweled gold cross hung from a chain around his neck.

He raised both hands, outstretched as if about to conduct an orchestra, and said, "Welcome to the Church of Faithful Followers."

"Good morning, Father," the crowd recited in unison.

"And why are we here?" asked Baldy.

"To find the way," they responded.

I glanced at James and saw he was struggling to stifle a grin. "Glad we're in the back row," I whispered.

Baldy was about to launch into a litany when the foyer doors burst open with a crash. The heads of the parishioners swivelled to the rear of the room, as if they were one. The intruder was dressed in camouflage gear and a black mask covered his face. "Find the way? I'll show you the way. The way to Hell! That's where sinners go, right Reverend?" Repent now!" he commanded.

It was the gun clasped in his left hand that held me frozen, totally in shock. Holy shit! This was a real gun, not a cigarette lighter shaped like one, and the guy was only a few feet away. Things were about to get ugly.

"And you, you sleazebag, you'll be the first to go!" shouted the man holding the gun. His hand shook. He marched down the aisle to get closer. He fired a shot at Baldy. Smoke puffed from the muzzle, and the blast reverberated in the room. I clutched my ears. My body felt numb, unable to move. My brain wasn't processing. Everything seemed to happen in slow motion, even though it was only seconds.

The statue of Mary teetered, and her left breast exploded as shards of plaster erupted. James pushed me to the floor and covered my body with his. I was flat on my stomach, and his heartbeat thundered against my back. It was a slow and steady rhythm. Damn, was this guy ever afraid of anything?

"Stay down," his voice sounded gruff.

From my vantage point on the floor, my face squished against the linoleum, I saw black running shoes as the intruder raced from the room. Doors flung open. Banged shut. An acrid odour filled my nostrils.

Shrieks of terror filled the room. Through the microphone from the front, I heard, "I've been shot. God help me, I've been shot!" The voice was panic-stricken, filled with pain. It was Baldy, the minister.

From two rows ahead, I recognized Bambi's voice. "Harold, Harold, I'm coming to you. Don't you fucking die on me!"

So Baldy's name was Harold.

I felt James's weight ease off my body, and I started to get up. "Stay down," he cautioned. "Let me check things out first."

Yeah right, like I ever followed directions. I was almost tripping on the heels of his shoes as he raced to the front of the church, towards the Harold, the minister. Mostly we had to fight our way up the aisle as everyone else rushed for an emergency exit.

Baldy, a.k.a. Harold, lay on the floor with a crimson flow of blood emanating from his left buttock and soaking through his white robe. He must have turned away when he saw the shooter. Shards of Mary's left breast were embedded in his buttock through the robe. Bambi cradled his head. James was already on the phone calling 911.

James looked at me. "Thought I told you to stay behind. Never mind, since you're here, put some pressure on the area to stop the bleeding. I'm going after the shooter."

Wonderful, I thought, *just wonderful*. I'd only ever seen the minister three times, and now it looked like I'd be seeing his behind for the second time. On this occasion, I might have to actually touch it. God, I would have killed for a pair of disposable gloves.

"Be careful, James," I shouted. He was already gone.

Aside from Bambi and Harold, I was the only person left in the room. Harold moaned as I gently eased the robe up to check out the wounds. Christ, he was as naked as a jaybird underneath. Didn't ministers wear underwear? At any rate, it was easier to see the damage this way. There were three shards firmly stuck in his left buttock, and the bleeding appeared to be slowing down to a trickle. I'd done a first-aid course before and knew the best thing to do was leave the offending pieces of Mary's breast in place. If I pulled them out, the bleeding could increase.

Bambi's voice trembled. "Harold, Harold, you know I love you. Please be okay. Promise me you'll be okay."

"My ass hurts," he groaned. "Who the hell was that guy? Why me?"

"It's okay, Harold. This lady will help you." She glanced up at me, and it took her a moment to register. "You, you, again."

I nodded. "It's complicated. Once Harold's safe, I'll explain."

For the second time in twelve hours, I heard the blaring sound of sirens. The foyer doors crashed open as paramedics rushed a stretcher into the church. They checked Harold's vital signs and strapped an oxygen mask on him. They told him he'd be fine, packed some gauze around the wounds, and loaded him onto the stretcher, belly down. At least they wouldn't have to transport him in an elevator, where surely they'd have to crank up one end of the stretcher to make it fit. And that would have been impossible with Harold lying on his stomach. And of course, there were no stairs to have to carry him down.

Bambi looked like a lost soul as they transported Harold to the ambulance. My heart went out to her. She obviously loved this guy for whatever reason. I needed to help her.

"Should you go with him? I can drive you if you want?" I asked.

"I can't. He's married. At least I think he still is, and what if his wife shows up?" She hung her head and sobbed.

13

Whiskey Makes Me Frisky,
LUKE BRYAN

Bambi was still shaking as I led her from the church and into the sports bar next door. We'd just been through of slew of questions from the police, and I knew I had a lot of explaining to do. Perhaps an adult beverage or two would make it easier. Besides, I could get a lot of valuable information from her. First, I needed to gain her trust. The whole chapter from my course on interviewing and interrogating seemed to have escaped me for the moment. No worries, I'd just make it up as I went along.

It was only five minutes past noon, and we were the only patrons. It made me think that the whole *happy hour starting at noon* gig wasn't really working for the bar.

"You're not who you pretended to be at the bar the other night, are ya?" Bambi asked.

"Not exactly," I said. "But first, I know you're worried about Harold. Trust me, they were only flesh wounds. He should be just fine."

We hauled ourselves up on a couple of bar stools. I was looking at the draft taps. Bambi, however, was eying the top shelf lined with liquor bottles. She glanced at me and asked, "You're paying?"

"Absolutely," I replied.

Bambi nodded at the bartender. "Jack Daniels and make it a double, water back, and hold the ice."

I didn't want to be outdone, so I said, "Make that two."

The bartender eyed us with a somewhat surprised expression. The bar had just opened, and he had two middle-aged ladies drinking the hard stuff. "Rough day already?" he asked.

"Trust me, ya don't wanna know," I said.

"Does this have anything to do with the fracas next door at the church?" he asked. "The cops have been all over the place."

"Just get the drinks, will ya," I said.

He grabbed the bottle, poured the shots, and quickly produced two glasses of water. I had to admit, he was a far cry from Teddy, the bartender at the Muff Dive—this guy was more like a retired pudgy imbiber.

Bambi took a slug of whiskey, swivelled expertly on her bar stool, and turned to face me. "Well then, Lucy, you got some major 'splaining to do." Who the hell was Lucy? Then I recognized the Desi Arnaz impersonation. Damn, she was good. After what she just witnessed, she still had a sense of humour, and it endeared her to me.

"Like I said, it's complicated. My name is Diana Darling, and I'm a private investigator. And no, I wasn't following you." That was partially the truth. James and I had been keeping tabs on Harold today.

I followed Bambi's lead, took a slurp of the Jack Daniels, and nearly coughed it back out. Clearly, you weren't supposed to drink this stuff like beer. I'd be more careful and sip next time.

"Well, someone's following me. If it isn't you, who is it?" she asked.

"Why do you think you're being followed?"

She ignored my question. "Now Harold's been shot, the bar's burned down, and I have no job. The only good news is that Harold got injured on the backside instead of the front."

Bambi clutched her glass, downed the double, skipped the water, and banged her glass on the bar. "Hit me again," she said, signalling the bartender.

"Should I just leave the bottle?" he asked as he slid a bowl of nuts and pretzels our way.

"Damned good idea," she said. "After all, she's paying."

I didn't want to think about how much a bottle of Jack Daniels was worth in a bar, but if I kept the receipt, James would have to cover it. At least Bambi had stopped shaking.

"Let me be honest here. I was hired by Harold's wife, Isadora. She thought he was having an affair." I cringed at how many privacy and confidentiality rules I was breaking, yet it seemed like the right thing to do. Besides, my client hadn't actually paid me yet, and there was nothing signed or in writing.

Bambi nodded. "But that doesn't explain the other guy. I remember him from the bar, a good tipper, and now he was in church with you. What in hell was he doing there?"

"His name is James. He's an ex-cop, now a private detective, and was hired by your husband, Nigel."

I caught the confused expression on her face. It only lasted an instant. This woman was smart. Her face reflected the pieces of a puzzle coming together, and I needed to give her time. I took another sip of whiskey.

"Okay, I think I'm getting it now," Bambi said. "Nigel's a first-class jerk. Not sure why I ever married him."

I nodded. "Sounds like my last ex-husband." Commiserating on previous spouses was always a solid link for women in our circumstances. This was good.

"Last ex-husband. How many have you had?" Bambi asked.

"Oh, I've had a couple of screw-ups. Not on my part, except for the maybe the last one." I clinked my glass against hers, proceeded to deliver some mumbo jumbo about smart women making bad choices, and waited.

"Sounds like we do have something in common then . . ." Bambi swirled the liquor in her glass before continuing. I figured she was wondering how much to share. I caught her hesitation just before she took another slurp.

"Carry on," I said and wished I hadn't left my spy camera pen in my car. How was I supposed to remember all this stuff? Gadgets are great, but only if you have them with you. Note to self: always be prepared.

"Nigel promised me a new life, lots of money; he said he loved me and all was good. It only lasted six months. Next thing I knew, he was pushing me for inside information on the patrons at the bar. I never figured he was using me to boost his career." Bambi's voice held a bitter tone.

"How so?" I asked.

She wiped a tear from her eye. "He takes advantage of seniors. Something Harold would never do. Harold's a good guy, even though he skims a bit from the collection plate at church. But it all goes to a shelter for abused women and their kids. That's why I love him."

That explains the earlier conversation I heard at the Muff Dive, when she'd said, "Make sure it's a good collection plate tomorrow." Wow, I had totally misjudged this woman.

The more she divulged, the sorrier I felt for her. Seniors can be a vulnerable population, and apparently Nigel had a habit of developing potential real estate, selling, and collecting cash for retirement home units that would never be built. He was also one of those guys that promised if he couldn't sell your home in thirty days, he'd buy it from you. Seniors were targets for being ripped off, and Nigel was taking full advantage, thanks to Bambi's inside information and connections.

"How'd you end up meeting Nigel?" I reached inside my purse, searching for a pad and pen to take notes. Nada. Crap, I'd have to rely on my memory.

"He showed up at the bar one night when I was working. A guy I'd found on the Meet Your Match website, who wanted to meet me. Guess I was feeling lonely. How could I have been so stupid?" She poured another drink and topped mine up too.

"So what about Harold? Where does he fit in the picture?" I asked.

She paused as if considering her response, then propped her head on the bar with both hands and shrugged. "Reckon I felt guilty. Went to church and that's where I met him. He was like a breath of fresh air compared to Nigel. Harold just seemed so honest. Didn't know he was married at the time, and he said he was trying to get out of it."

I may have quit my number crunching job, but I still carried my skills, knew about scam artists like Nigel, and even helped some of their targets get out of crisis situations. This seemed like the right time to help another woman, and besides, I was developing a soft spot for Bambi. Maybe it was a result of me causing her lack of employment because of that lit cigarette that burned the joint down. Or maybe it was the half-downed bottle of Jack

Daniels. Most likely, it was because she had a heart. And it was a good one.

An hour later, I was reeling from the amount of information I had on Nigel. Also reeling from the liquor, even though I remembered to drink the water. She reassured me she didn't recognize the shooter, so it was definitely not Nigel.

Leaving Bambi at the bar, I made my way to the ladies room, settled myself on the porcelain chamber, and winced at the one-ply toilet paper. After hauling a yard's worth of toilet paper out, I did my business, washed my hands, and staggered back to the bar. Crap, I was feeling guilty. I knew I couldn't afford to pay Bambi, but damn she'd be a great receptionist. And if she had half of the social network she said she did, that would be awesome, even if it included the senior biker gang as customers. Plus, I pretty much convinced myself that she wasn't a killer.

"Here's the deal," I said when I returned to the bar stool. "I feel like we've made a connection. I know you're out of a job, and I could sure use a smart woman like you." Nothing like building up her ego; in reality, everything I said was true. "I need a receptionist, just temporarily. Can't pay you, but I'll give you a percentage on any cases you bring in."

"How long ya been in business?" Bambi asked. Her voice was starting to sound a bit slurred, but hell, so was mine.

"Long enough," I said. No sense getting carried away with telling the truth now.

We clinked our glasses.

"Trust me," said Bambi. "I can steer some business your way. Plus, I can give you stuff on Nigel that your other guy, that good-looking hunk of mash-culinity, would take years to find out."

"How so?" I asked.

"He kicked me out of the house a couple weeks ago. Since then Harold and I've been living at the Whispering Pines motel. You know it?" Bambi asked.

I nodded. "So Harold moved out of his house to live with you?"

"More like his wife kicked him out. Same day, Nigel booted me out. Coincidence you think?"

Even my alcohol-induced brain managed to make some sense of this. "Unlikely," I said. "So what have ya got?"

"I still have a spare key to his house. Pretty sure I could get inside and copy the hard drive of his computer onto a memory stick. It could be some interesting reading material. So are you giving me a job or what? I can have a lineup of customers outside your door by tomorrow."

I really wasn't sure what a memory stick was. Presumed it was like a floppy disk and something I could figure out on my own.

"You're hired," I said. "Here's my card. We can work out the details later."

I waved at the bartender and caught him wince. When he realized I was asking for the bill instead of a refill for the bottle, he looked relieved. "How 'bout I call you ladies a cab?" It wasn't so much a question as a statement.

There was no way I was in any condition to drive, and a cab sounded good. Bambi and I stumbled out of the bar, thankful there were no stairs. My head was doing that spinning thing, and fortunately I got dropped off first. Bambi had my business card and said she'd meet me in the morning.

I staggered into my office, tripped over Xena, and fell onto my bed. The red digital numbers of my alarm clock glared at me. Hell, it was only three o'clock in the afternoon. I still had a good case of the spins, so I threw my left leg over the edge of the bed to rest on the floor. There was something to be said for grounding, and back in my teens, after I would over imbibe, this method had worked.

But this time it didn't. Three minutes later, my stomach was chatting with the big white porcelain telephone in the bathroom. My throat felt like I'd just hurled battery acid, my abs were killing me, and Xena was twirling around my ankles, reminding me she needed food.

On hands and knees, I crawled to the fridge, extracted a Friskies tin, tore off the lid, and let her eat it out of the can.

That's when the phone rang. I struggled to stand upright, staggered to the desk, and gingerly held the phone to my pounding head. It was James.

"I lost him," he said. "Just checking to make sure you got home okay."

Lost who? I thought, then I remembered the whole fiasco from earlier. The last time I saw James, he'd been running after the shooter out of the church. It seemed like a lifetime ago.

"Diana?" he asked. "Are you still there?"

"Yup," I needed to keep my verbiage to single words. That way, I'd have less a chance of slurring.

"Meet me at my office in the morning. We'll go over the case files. In the meantime, keep your doors locked," he said.

"Suure thing," I mumbled and hung up.

I knew I'd given Bambi my business card. And now I was second guessing myself. Had I also given her a spare key to my office when we were in the back seat of the cab? What in hell had I done?

14

Annie Get Your Gun,
OVERTURE BY SUZI QUATRO

It was the morning after the church circus event, and James paced his office, restless, with an open file folder in one hand. I already knew that the shooter had escaped, and there was an all-points police bulletin for his immediate arrest.

"We're missing something here," James said.

"Like what?" I asked.

Silence filled the room. I wasn't sure if he heard me or not, so decided to just shut up and wait. This was the first time I'd been in his office, and it was an office that I would have killed for. Given the location in the lucrative business district of town, he probably attracted the type of clients I could only dream of. A receptionist who looked like a model, a conference room capable of seating at least a dozen people, and a fully equipped kitchen and bathroom that included a shower and a walk-in closet. James was the real deal. Not like me, who put up a storefront façade in a strip mall and lived in the back of the office.

"Maybe we're looking at this from the wrong angle," I suggested tentatively. My earlier vow to remain silent reminded me I wasn't very good at following my own rules.

"What do you mean?" He stopped pacing and turned to face me.

"We've been presuming Bambi and Harold are the bad guys. What if they're not?"

"Continue," he said.

"What if it's Isadora and Nigel behind all this?"

"Why would you think that?"

The tone in his voice spurred me on. James sounded non-judgmental, open to thinking outside the box, still I hesitated before speaking. "Look at the facts. The only people that have been injured or compromised are Harold and Bambi. Someone shot Harold in broad daylight in a church, and Bambi thinks she's being followed," I said.

"What do you mean she thinks she's being followed? When did you find that out?" James asked.

"Oh, just a conversation we had after the shooting yesterday. Sorry, James, I didn't have a chance to tell you before."

His cheek was doing that tweaking thing again, and his face was deep in concentration.

I plunged ahead. "Have you heard from your client and has he paid you?"

"Nope." James stopped pacing. "Have you heard from yours?"

"Nothing. So if Isadora and Nigel are missing, that just doesn't make sense. What if they know each other and decided to get rid of their respective spouses? What if they hired us to cover their tracks? What if they wanted to make Bambi and Harold out to be the bad guys?" I asked.

Crap, how come I couldn't keep my lips zippered shut? Even to me, this sounded really far-fetched. If I kept this up, pretty soon he'd be thinking I was as crazy as his ex-wife.

"Mmm, I never thought about it that way. I suppose it's worth a deeper background check to see if there's any connection. The town's not that big, and it's possible they know each other," James said.

I could practically see the wheels turning in his head. No grinding of gears, just a smooth hum of a finely honed machine. This time, I was determined to keep quiet and let him digest the information. He settled into a mammoth leather chair behind his desk, arms crossed behind his head as he thought.

"But . . ." I hesitated.

"But what?" he asked.

"There was something about that shooter. I just can't put my finger on it. There was something familiar about him. Just one of those niggling feelings, like getting a song stuck in your head and you can't delete it," I said.

Most people have five senses; the sixth one is intuition. Some people have a seventh sense, and that was the one intruding on my brain. I practically gnawed through my tongue by the time James finally spoke again. At least there wasn't any blood this time.

"Okay, here's the deal. Let's do a . . ." He was interrupted by a light tap on the door. "Come in, Melanie."

"Sorry to interrupt, sir. You have an urgent call on line three. The person said they couldn't wait. They need to speak with you immediately about the church shooting."

Melanie's perfectly made-up face gave me a quizzical look up and down, as if she wondered what I was doing there. I sat up straight in my chair, smoothed my Wally Mart blouse down the front, and wondered if perhaps the coffee stain hadn't been fully removed.

"I can take the lady to the waiting room if you need some privacy?" Her voice sounded condescending, and it bugged me to no end.

"Thanks, Mel, I'll take it. Ms. Darling will remain here." He waited until she left the room before he picked up the phone and answered, "Woods here."

Wow, James considered me important enough to stay. I secretly smiled as Melanie left the room, and I particularly loved the confused expression on her face as she closed the door. Melanie was probably wondering who the chick in the cheap clothes was and why she was allowed to stay.

I listened intently to the one-sided phone conversation. At one point, James got up from his desk and strode across the room to stare out the window. "What the fuck?" he said. A few seconds later, "That's a quick turnaround for prints." He brushed his hand through his hair, turning to glance at me. "Yes, yes, of course I'll keep you posted if anything turns up from my end. Thanks for the scoop."

He returned the phone to its charger, plunked down into his chair, spun it around, and let out a loud *whoop*! My mind was racing at breakneck speed, dying to know what was going on, but then he reached across the desk and grabbed both of my hands. "Diana Darling, you are one smart cookie."

"Huh?" I asked.

"That was my cop friend who's the lead investigator of the church shooting. They found the shooter's ski mask and the gun in a garbage dumpster about ten blocks away."

"Okay, that's good." I still couldn't figure out what was going on, yet it sounded like good news, or so I hoped. Besides, I loved the feel of his hands on mine.

"You mentioned something earlier about the shooter? Something you couldn't quite put your finger on. What do you remember about him?"

Mostly I remembered James lying on top of me. Even though my face was squished against the floor, his body had felt nice—full contact, except for the clothes between us. I reeled in my meandering thoughts before speaking. "Well, first of all, he's left-handed, wears size ten running shoes, and has really bad taste in clothes. Camouflage gear went out of style a few years back. Oh, and he must be really stupid if he ditched the gun near the scene."

"What about the voice? Anything you recall?" James inquired.

"He sounded like he might be trying to disguise his voice. Maybe a little glib. Kind of a mesmerizing tone mixed in with some commands, almost like he was used to being on stage."

My brain was starting to hurt from too much thinking. Or maybe it was from all the alcohol I had to drink with Bambi yesterday. That's when the light bulb went on in my head. That eureka moment when everything comes crashing together. It was a brilliant feeling. The shooter's voice belonged to Andrew, the couples retreat counsellor that James and I had busted a mere week ago for blackmailing women. I remembered that slime ball handing me a glass of champagne in the hot tub—it was in his left hand.

"It's Andrew, isn't it?" I asked.

"Right again. His fingerprints were all over the gun, and with his felony background, he was already in the system. Never pegged him for a shooter though."

"Did they catch him?"

"Nah, he's still at large for now. So let's get back to your earlier thoughts. I'm beginning to think you're right. At the very least, it's worth following up to see if there's a connection with Isadora and Nigel."

I nodded. I'd like to think there was a new tone of respect in James's voice, or maybe it was just wishful thinking. His next statement was totally out of the blue and caught me off guard. "Do you have a gun?" he asked.

"Nope. Do I need one?" The very thought of holding a gun in my hand made me shudder. My mother had always been a fan of bows and arrows. "Less-life threatening and harder to hit the target," my mother had always said.

"With Andrew on the loose, it might be safer for you," James said. He rifled through his desk drawer and handed me a business card. "Here's the address for a shooting range. I'll meet you there tomorrow morning at 9:00 a.m. for practice. We can work out the gun purchase and licence later."

Wow! This was so much more exciting than working as a number cruncher. I, Diana Darling, was about to become armed and dangerous. What a rush!

"Just one more detail," James said. "I'm worried about Bambi. You said she thought she was being followed. Any chance you can contact her just to follow up and make sure she's okay?"

"No problem." I didn't think it was the right time to tell him I already had it covered. After all, Bambi was about to become my new part-time receptionist. James would find out when the time was right.

15

Friends in Low Places,
GARTH BROOKS

On the way home, I stopped to do some shopping and then arrived outside my office to find that someone had filled the three parking spaces that were supposedly mine. The property manager had warned me it frequently happened on the weekends when the business next door, a children's birthday party trampoline franchise, was loaded with customers. Today was only Wednesday and mid-afternoon. What the hell was going on? I thrust my car into reverse, found a vacant spot a few doors down, grabbed my groceries, and hefted a twenty-pound bag of cat litter over my shoulder.

    I struggled to reach my office door, and that's when the proverbial penny dropped. One of the spaces was occupied by a Harley-Davidson with a handicap sticker on the back. Whoa, it had to be Dave from the strip club. Parked beside the bike was an ancient turquoise Pontiac Parisienne that I also recognized from the club. Plus, the third space was occupied by Harold's convertible

Mustang. Bambi had said she'd bring me business. It was obvious I'd underestimated her. Also it confirmed my earlier question: yup, I must have given her a key.

The three folding chairs in my waiting room were filled for the first time since I opened my investigative agency. Tribal Tits was there with a new short hairdo, cropped to her ears and fluffy, a.k.a. no hairspray. Dave's fold-up walker leaned against the wall, and in the third seat was, Oh My God, Teddy the bartender with the chocolate eyes. I struggled to focus.

"Hey, Diana. Brought you some customers." Bambi's voice came from behind the reception desk, bringing me back to reality as I wrestled to erase the image of the bartender and me at a nude beach somewhere in the Caribbean.

"Thanks, Bambi. I'll just put these things away, and we can get down to business." It was her first day on the job, she'd taken charge, and I was impressed. Who needed Della Street when you had Bambi?

She met me in my private office and produced three file folders. "The first person you need to see is Deborah."

"Huh," I said. *Who's Deborah?* I wondered.

"Deb's the stripper. Apparently she and her twin sister were adopted at birth by two separate families. Now she wants to find her. I've assured her you're a professional and will help."

I didn't recall learning anything in my course about how to find a lost person, but perhaps I could figure it out. Before I could respond, Bambi was already saying, "I watch those TV shows about finding missing people all the time, and I've already started a search for her using social media. Just spend a couple of minutes with Deb. Let her know you're on the case and then she's free to go."

A few minutes later, a satisfied Deborah exited my office. This time, her breasts seemed to be held up by a very substantial bra, probably made of a ton of underwire mesh. I reckoned her breasts exited the room a full three seconds before the rest of her body. Since both of the implants seemed intact, I presumed the security guard hadn't punctured one of them.

The next case was Dave, the walker-wielding Harley driver. Bambi pulled out his file. "It was a work-related injury three years ago," Bambi said. "Dave was loading pumpkins onto a wagon when one rolled off and crushed him. He's been on disability ever since because of the back injury. Now the insurance company is questioning his claim."

"Why now?" I asked.

"Seems they're looking at his income from the club he set up a couple of years back, and they're also wondering how he's still able to ride a bike. He told them he needs the walker to get around."

"Must have been one hell of a pumpkin," I said.

Bambi gave me a lopsided grin. "Well, according to Dave, it took first place in some contest."

Holy crap, what was I supposed to do with this case? I paused, then nodded at Bambi. "This won't be my first dance with insurance companies," I lied. "I'm sure we can work something out for him. Just let him know it's going to take time." *And money*, I thought. Maybe I'd need James's help with this one.

With Dave's meeting over, I watched as he used the walker to stroll through the door, then he folded it, strapped it onto the back of his Harley, and easily rode away. He made me wonder about ethics and insurance fraud.

"Ready for the next customer?" Bambi asked as she fanned her face with the file folder before tossing it on the desk.

Boy, was I ever. It was the bartender with the eyes to kill for, and I realized his effect on Bambi too. "This is Teddy, and he's reasonably new at the bar. All the staff love him, and he's a big reason the bar turns the profit it does. The blue rinse older ladies just keep coming back. I reckon they're not there to look at the stripper. Mind you, he's a hit with the guys too," Bambi said.

Oh, oh, did that mean he was gay? My heart was almost crushed until she said, "Teddy's ex-wife is screwing him over for child support. He's not even sure the kid is his, and the ex-wife refuses to do any DNA testing."

"Wow, you're really good at this stuff," I said.

"Trust me, I may not have a lot of schooling, but I'm street smart, and that has to count for something. Besides, all we need to do is collect some snot from the kid and send it to a lab. How hard can that be?"

"Send him in," I said. My office suddenly felt a lot smaller as Teddy entered.

"I knew there was something about you I liked," he said as he flashed a smile at me. "I just didn't figure you for a private dick."

I pretended to peruse the file, but even under the harsh fluorescent lighting, he still looked amazing. He gave me a rambling version of his brief encounter with his ex-wife. He met her online, one of those Meet Your Match websites, and after six months of chatting and a quick visit from her, he moved from the Cayman Islands to the US just to be with her. The kid arrived eight months later, and his ex-wife had said the baby was premature.

"I'm just not sure the kid is mine, and now she's hitting me up for money," Teddy said.

"Teddy," I smiled. "I'm happy to take you on as a client. It may take a while for me to investigate your case though."

He offered his hand and shook mine, holding on for too long, and I struggled not to blush. The longer I could keep him as a client, the better. Even if it was just to go swimming in those mesmerizing eyes.

Reluctantly, I watched as he left my office. I swooned at his firm, round behind in those tight jeans and the natural swagger to his walk. Man, he was the total package—definite lipstick removal material.

Bambi was soon back. "Okay, so I've unpacked your groceries, changed the cat litter, and cleared the waiting room. Anything else you need before I go for the day?"

"Nope, good job today. By the way I'll be out tomorrow morning for a bit. You okay with coming in on your own, opening up the shop, answering calls?"

"Diana, I've noticed you don't seem to have a lot of business aside from what I've brought you today, so yes of course." Yuck, she already knew me too well.

"Oh, and by the way," she said. "I snuck inside Nigel's place last night when he was out. Found the spare key under a garden gnome, copied the stuff from his computer, and left the memory stick in your top right-hand drawer. I'm not really sure what's on it. Maybe it's nothing after all."

Before leaving the office, she gave Xena a quick pat and promised she'd return in the morning with treats for her "special kitty." My feline nuzzled Bambi's cheek in return, mounted the cat tree, and stared longingly in her direction after the door closed. That darned cat!

In the meantime, there was homework to do, as in figuring out that damned memory stick. The memory stick looked about the size of one of those pink pencil erasers that came apart when I pulled on it. Okay, so it looked like it should plug into the side of the computer.

After a few tries, success appeared on my screen, and I did a quick scroll through. There were tons of files, and I only skimmed a few. A couple of them were personal, so I'd save those for later, including the porn sites he obviously visited on a frequent basis. Some files were like reading a diary of activities, but the ones that really caught my eye were those related to banking, investing, and accounting practices. The files were there, but when I tried to access them, they required a password. I printed off a few sheets for James, just enough to give him the drift of Nigel's activities, and decided to call it a day.

A few hours later, I was sifting through my closet. Hmm, what does one wear to a shooting range?

16

Hit Me with Your Best Shot,
PAT BENATAR

Where the hell was this place? I double-checked the address on the business card James had given me. Maybe shooting ranges were designed to be off the beaten path. Probably safer for the people who lived nearby. Yet here I was, in the middle of bumfuck nowhere, looking for a place called Shooters. I eased my car to the side of the gravel road to check the map when I heard the sound of gunfire. *Bang, Bang!* Then a male voice shouted, "Hey, looks like you got that one. Great aim, Buddy!"

I've never been to a shooting range before, and according to my online research, this place had both an indoor and outdoor range. Obviously I found the outdoor range first. As I continued driving, I really hoped Buddy had a good shot. The last thing I wanted was a stray bullet coming through my car. I rolled my window closed, just in case.

The next lane up steered me towards a building that looked like a bowling alley, or given the rural location, it could have been a really long pig barn. It was a low one-story structure made of dismal grey concrete and a painted sign that read, *Shooters*. I had arrived. James's Jeep was already parked in the lot. I wondered why he'd picked this remote location. Did it mean he didn't trust me to be armed?

My only experience with shooters were the high-octane alcohol ones served in bars—my favourite being a mix of vodka, Frank's red hot sauce, a splash of clamato juice, and a pickled green bean. It was known as Knock 'Em Dead. Since I was at a shooting range, it seemed appropriate.

I was afraid to look up at the sky, just in case Mom was looking down at me. She'd probably be giving me a questioning look and saying, "Okay, perhaps I can understand you being at the strip bar. Perhaps I can forgive you for marrying those jerks, but really, do you need a gun, dear?" I was relieved to see the sky was overcast; odds were Mom would not be able to see me.

Last night I'd practiced, even posing with a pretend gun in the mirror, trying to emulate one of Charlie's Angels. In the midst of tossing my flowing auburn hair over my shoulder, whilst I tried to do a twist and turn, I tripped over my cat. The gun, an open stapler, landed in the sink with a clatter. Xena had not been impressed and showed her displeasure by peeing outside the litter box. My cat has a mind of her own, kind of like me. I guess that's why we mostly get along.

I closed the door of my car, avoided looking at the sky, and made a mental note to get a second litter box for Xena, just in case she was taken short.

Inside the building, I was greeted by a middle-aged man, who looked as if his face should be on a wanted poster; probably had been at some point in his life.

"Welcome to Shooters," he said. "I'm Rambo, the range master."

If Rambo was really his name, then I sure as hell needed to see my optometrist real soon. For me, the name was reserved for Sylvester Stallone, and him only. The only muscular part of this guy's body seemed to be his overdeveloped elbows. Perhaps a side effect of lifting too many brewskies to the lips. His eyes were too close together. He was unshaven, at least six inches shorter than me, and looked like he'd just crawled off a couch somewhere.

Rambo made me read a bunch of stuff that seemed ridiculous. I could understand that the safety lecture was necessary, but I also had to sign a waiver for any damages. What in hell was that all about? After all, it was a shooting range. There were bound to be bullet holes left somewhere.

"Why are you here?" he asked.

"It's a shooting range, isn't it? I want to learn how to shoot," I said.

He rolled his eyes before continuing, "Have you ever fired a gun before?"

"Nope, this will be my first time," I said, tilting my head down to stare at him. At my age, there weren't many activities where I could consider myself a virgin. When it came to guns, this would definitely be my first. Also, I didn't have many chances to look down at a man. It made me want to stand straighter, pulling myself up to reach my full five feet, two and a half inches of height. I loved it!

"Make sure you only aim down the alley," Rambo said.

Like duh! Where else would I be aiming? If this guy was really the range master, I wondered where he'd gotten his credentials.

"Oh, and you can pick your own target," he said. "I'll add it to the bill." He laid out a spreadsheet that covered everything from Hello Kitty to wildlife outlines and political figures. Another two were labelled ex-wife or ex-husband, and the final few were the usual profiles I'd seen on TV: the ambiguous figure with just the torso outlined. Given Xena's behaviour last night, I was tempted to go for the kitty one.

Rambo handed me a pair of safety goggles, ear plugs, and earmuffs to put on. Oh joy, I was about to become deaf. I guessed James and I would be communicating through sign language, but it wasn't like we hadn't done it before. Rambo pointed at a display cabinet. Everything from small ladylike pistols to guns I'd seen James Bond use in his 007 movies. Was I supposed to pick one?

The door to the range opened, and I was relieved to see James. A waft of cordite filled my nostrils, and the unmistakable sound of gunfire pierced through the heavy double doors.

"Glad you could make it, Diana." Then he addressed Rambo. "The lady's with me. I'll look after everything."

Mmm, I thought. James could definitely take care of everything as far as I was concerned.

"Yes of course, Mr. Woods. No problem. The ammunition is free for the both of you." Rambo's tone went from zero to sixty in terms of respect, and it had only taken a nanosecond.

James selected a gun. "This is a 9 mm Glock, with nine bullets in the clip. There's no hammer. You'll just have to fire," he explained as he walked me through the double doors.

There were ten lanes inside the indoor range, and eight were already occupied. James had already been practicing, and his target was ripped with shots within a six-inch radius of its heart. Damn, this guy was good.

He placed the gun in my hand. Cold metal, a bit heavy, and I could hardly wait. My heart rate was somewhere just below stroke level.

"Think about your target first. Now, stretch your arm out," James said.

"Like this, James?" I really wanted him to come closer, adjust my stance, but it wasn't happening.

"Flex your elbow just a bit," he said. "That's perfect. Now hold your hand steady, support your elbow, and aim. Fire when you're ready."

It sounded easy enough. As I squeezed the trigger, the recoil sent my arm flying upwards. Pain reverberated through my shoulder and into my neck. Crap, my first shot took out a ceiling light. Dust filtered down, and the lane was now a tad darker. That was okay with me. Perhaps it was karma, a test to see how I was at night shooting, and would enable me to be better prepared.

James's cheek was doing that tweaking thing again, and I hated that he seemed to be stifling a smile. "Okay, let's try again," he said. At least I was pretty sure that's what he said. With the headgear, it was hard to hear. Nevertheless, it appeared obvious that I needed a do-over.

I overcompensated on my next shot and managed to upturn some dirt on the floor, below the target. Being armed and dangerous was not as easy as I'd anticipated, and apparently my practice with the stapler last night hadn't helped. But I've never been a person who gives up easily. I persisted, determined to shoot a bullet at the target.

The lanes were divided for the first few feet in front of me. Beyond that, they were wide open. The target was hung from the ceiling, and pressing a toggle switch moved it forward and backward. I moved my target up five feet, thinking that the closer the better. I imagined Andrew's face on the target. Aim, flex the elbow, breathe, and then fire.

My third shot went straight to the target's neck. Unfortunately, it was the target of the guy shooting in the lane next to me. Damn, I would have been better off with a bow and arrow!

I half-heard James's apologies and noticed the guy moved to the free lane furthest away from me.

After an hour, my arm ached from the shoulder down. My hand was numb, and so far, all I'd managed to hit was two ceiling lights, someone else's target, and I'd done major damage to the back wall and dirt floor in my alley.

James led me to the front office where I tore off the earmuffs and pulled out the ear plugs. "Okay, Diana, perhaps shooting isn't your forte," he said. "How about I arm you with some pepper spray, in the event you're near Andrew?"

It was hard to ignore the pained expression on his face, and it looked as if he'd chewed through half of his inner left cheek.

"Sounds good," I agreed. I am a realist after all, and if I hadn't impressed him at the shooting range, I had info that was sure to leave him reeling. "I've got some background info on Nigel. It's in a file folder in my car. You might find it an interesting read."

"That's great," he said. "I'll meet you in the parking lot. First, I'll need to settle up with Rambo for the damages to the ceiling lights."

I cringed. But after all, this whole gun shooting practice had been his idea. Not my problem. "Maybe you can recoup some cash on my virgin target. He can resell it," I said.

James simply smiled. At least I hoped it was a smile, instead of a grimace.

17

Hot Hot Hot,
ARROW

The sun broke through the clouds as I headed to my car. Probably Mom's way of saying, *glad you didn't buy a gun*. Our communication had always been unique. Not your average mother-daughter relationship. She was bulletproof, and nothing I'd ever done or said seemed to upset her. Not even the time I decked little Mikey Patterson in grade three. He'd called me a *nerd*. I wasn't even sure what *nerd* was, but since it didn't sound very nice, I punched him in the nose with my fist.

Mom had taken me to the hospital emergency room, and I left with a cast up to my elbow. Big cast for a fractured little finger. Anyways, she also pleaded my case with the school principal, and I got off with a week's detention after school. Mom was an intellectual type, always looked at the bigger picture, and never chastised me for mistakes I made, and I'd done plenty wrong. Mom was an awesome woman, and I missed her big time. This time, I dared to look up at the sky and gave her a silent salute.

I was opening my trunk to grab the file when James arrived. He tossed a can of pepper spray at me and said, "Just read the directions. Should be simple enough."

"No problem," I said. After all, it was only about the size of a sample can of hairspray. I could handle this.

"So what do you have on Nigel?" he asked.

"There's a synopsis on the front page. Give it a scan and let me know if you have any questions." It had taken me a whole two hours to figure out how to access stuff from the memory stick Bambi had given me.

While James read, I was busy reading the pepper spray instructions, which included *make sure you aim away from you,* when James erupted with a loud, "Holy shit! I had no idea what a bottom feeder this guy is. Where did you get this intel?"

I didn't think it was the right time to tell him most of it came from Bambi and the hard drive she copied from Nigel's computer. He flipped through a few more pages. "This is excellent!"

James picked me up and swung me around in the parking lot. I wrapped my arms around his neck, inhaled the Old Spice, and wished this moment could last forever. The can of pepper spray was still in my hand, and I accidentally poked myself in the eye with the trigger. It was just a little puff, but in seconds, hot blinding tears streamed down my cheeks. My eyes bubbled and boiled, and I had trouble breathing. Putting my feet back on the ground, James returned to the file folder, seemingly oblivious to my test run of the pepper spray. Thank God, he must have been facing downwind when it sprayed.

I wheezed. Grabbed at my eyes and wished I could duck my head into ice water somewhere in the Arctic Ocean. Damn, this stuff hurt. I turned away, not wanting him to see me like this, plus I was embarrassed as hell. Coordination both on and off the shooting range didn't seem to be within my karmic realm at the moment. I dashed the tears away, sure that the whites of my eyes looked like they'd just been rolled in the Knock 'Em Dead shot glass, dyed with clamato juice. I know one of the active ingredients in pepper spray is capsicum, normally found in chilies. Since I voluntarily downed them in shooters, I could survive this.

I was temporarily blind in one eye and squinted through the other. James was still reading the file. It was ten pages long, so I had enough time to retrieve a pair of sunglasses from my car, then I had a few more minutes to recover. Thank God for the cool breeze that cleared my tears.

James turned to the last page of the file folder as I wiped my face with my sleeve. His cell phone rang, "Woods here." There was a pause, then he said, "Excellent," as he turned to look at me. "Keep the pepper spray with you at all times, just in case. Andrew's just used his credit card at a convenience store. I'm going to check it out."

Before heading off, he said, "Are you alright, Diana? Something seems off."

"Yeah, I'm okay," I managed to say.

His cheek was doing the tweaking thing again. I had the feeling he knew about my little test run with the pepper spray; still he was giving me the benefit of the doubt. "Just one thing, with the pepper spray, make sure you aim away from you. That stuff hurts like hell! I'll meet you at your office later," he added. "Keep your cell phone with you."

"Sure, James." *Wonderful, just wonderful*, I thought as I climbed into my Hyundai. I shoved the offending pepper spray into the glove compartment and hoped there were still a few dregs left in the wine box in my fridge 'cause I'd sure be in need of them.

I made sure James had at least a fifteen-minute head start before I headed out of the parking lot of Shooters. My eyes still burned as I squinted and rubbed them while driving down the lane. Buddy was still shouting, "Great shot, man," and it made me wonder how much time people spent at shooting ranges. Perhaps for some, it was a hobby. As for me, it seemed like a one-off deal. Guns were obviously not my thing. The Kleenex box on the passenger seat was now empty thanks to all the tears I'd shed from the pepper spray, and I couldn't wait to get home.

The parking spaces outside my office were empty except for a recognizable 1967 Mustang convertible. Hmm, Bambi must have borrowed Harold's car. As I walked through the front door, Xena barely gave me a nod, instead curled up on the desk and looked longingly at the lady on the phone.

"Yes, of course," Bambi was saying to the caller. "Diana Darling is the best, and I'm sure she'll be able to help you out." Bambi glanced at me, frowned, shook her head, held a cautionary finger at her lips, and said, "I'll have her call you back. She's not in the office right now."

Huh, what was she thinking? I was standing right in front of her.

"Good Lord. What in hell happened to you? You look like your eyes were marinated in tomato juice."

"I'm fine. Just rubbed my eyes with something I'm allergic to. An antihistamine will fix it, so no problem." She didn't look as if she believed me, so it was time to change the subject. "Isn't that Harold's car outside? How's he doing?"

The diversion seemed to have worked.

"Well he's out of the hospital. Still has to sleep on his side and has trouble sitting in a chair. Otherwise, all is good," she replied.

"His wife, Isadora, never even showed up to see him. Guess she didn't love him as much as I do."

I wanted to say that Isadora had never responded to my calls, and the last time I called, the voice message said, "The voice mail box for this recipient is full." It made me wonder where she was.

"Tell you what, why don't you take the rest of the day off," I said.

"That works, besides Harold needs some antibiotic cream applied to his . . ." she hesitated, "his wounds."

"Before you go, what about the caller on the phone? Anything I need to follow up on?"

"Nah, don't think so. She sounded like a crazy lady. Rambled on about being kidnapped by her husband and medicated against her will. Said her name was Tricky or Nikki, or something that sounded like that. She'll call you tomorrow."

On her way to the door, she paused. "You might want to get call display, you know. That way, you can avoid answering unwanted calls."

She left, and I headed to the fridge. It sounded like James's ex was a persistent soul. I'd deal with her tomorrow. Wine time was overdue. I hauled out the box and poured a glass. Life was good!

18

The Heat Is On,
GLENN FREY

Two hours later, my cell phone rang. I was about to launch into my *fake-receptionist* introduction when I realized the only person who had this phone number was James.

"Do ya wanna ... see ... live ... dead ... again?" The reception on my phone was sketchy, and the speaker kept cutting in and out. The caller must have been driving through a tunnel, or perhaps it was a telemarketer in a far away country, like Timbuktu, trying to sell me something I didn't want or need. I couldn't even determine if the voice was male or female. Probably some drunk with the wrong number on speed dial, or probably someone who wanted me to purchase life insurance, duct cleaning, or pre-arrange my own funeral.

But then again, it was a call on the burner phone from James. How had anyone even found this number? The compact gadget was a myriad of buttons, and I frantically searched to figure out which key to push to end the call. Sometimes technology can be a real pain in the ass.

"James wouldn't be happy if you hung up on me." This time the voice was clear, sharp, and definitely male.

It took a few seconds, before my brain synapses snapped into place, and I recognized the caller. It was Andrew. I decided to play dumb. Sometimes that's easy for me, plus I needed time to figure out why he was calling me and why James wouldn't be happy.

"Who are you?" I asked.

"Give me a break, Diana. You know damn well who this is."

Obviously my dumb act wasn't going anywhere. I manufactured my best authoritative tone and demanded, "Okay, Andrew, if he's there with you, put him on the phone."

"James can't come to the phone right now." Andrew's singsong tone, as if recording a voice mail, made my belly churn. In fact, it scared the bejesus out of me.

"Your buddy is kinda out of commission," Andrew continued. His voice raised my hackles. I pictured him with his overbleached Chiclet teeth and fake tan—the image clear in my mind. He was like a bad rash that wouldn't go away.

The last time I talked to James, he said, "Andrew just used his credit card at a convenience store. I'm heading there. In the meantime, stay safe and keep the damned pepper spray with you." That had only been an hour ago. Now James was in trouble, big trouble, by the sound of it.

"Andrew, where are you?" I asked.

"I'll tell you. But first, if I get even a sniff of any cops or you bring anyone else, James is a dead man."

"What have you done?" I struggled to keep my voice even.

Andrew continued, "Looks like the best of men can be knocked out by a stun gun. Mind you, he lasted longer than most. He may have hit his head on the way down. There's a bit of blood."

I fought to control my anger. Really wanted to call Andrew an *asshole*, but knew that would accomplish nothing. Instead, I hastily wrote down the address he gave me on a slip of paper. Good, it was only a few blocks away, at an abandoned warehouse—how cliché. I recognized the place immediately, but let him give me directions anyway. Stun guns weren't meant to kill, just temporarily disable, weren't they? I had no idea how long the effects lasted, but the longer I kept Andrew on the phone, the more time James had to recover.

"Andrew, why James? Why me? Why are you after us?" I already knew we'd destroyed his career as a counsellor at the couples retreat a few weeks back, but then he'd shown up with a gun in church and took a shot at Harold. There didn't seem to be a connection, and it seemed pretty far-fetched. I was still sifting through Nigel's file, and so far Andrew's name hadn't come up.

That's when he shouted, "Just get the hell here now. Otherwise, I'll shoot your friend. Or is he your lover? He kinda went all mushy when I mentioned your name." The sound of a gunshot blasted through the phone.

I gasped and heard Andrew do some fake moaning, followed by sinister laughter. "That was only for practice." *Click!* Then an empty hum on the phone was all I heard.

I was already out the door, in my car, and on my way. Some of the street lamps were burned out. It didn't matter because I knew the location by heart. My first part-time job during high school had been in that building, working at a bench where I would construct birdcage furniture, like little ladders and swings with bells on them. After a few years, you could actually graduate to cage design, sales, and marketing. Even with that sort of temptation, I chose to stay in school.

Thanks to Mom and her witchcraft business, I chose something on the opposite end of the spectrum: business and finance. But regardless, I knew every square inch of that building, including how to slip in and out undetected. It had been empty for the last few years, and the layout probably hadn't changed much since I worked there. Andrew may have expected me to enter through the front door. He had another thing coming.

I parked a block away, grabbed a flashlight from the trunk of my car, tucked the pepper spray into the waistband of my jeans, and headed to the rear of the building. In the alley, I was confronted by the sounds of wildlife. Bold eyes from a raccoon glimmered in the dark. Rats skittered away from my footfalls. But the biggest rat of all was inside. I couldn't wait to catch him.

Past the main shipping entrance at the back was a small side door. Way back then, the only people who used the side door were the staff who snuck outside for a smoke or the odd employee who didn't want to get nailed by the boss for being late. It was exactly as I remembered, since I'd been guilty on both counts.

I grabbed a used gift card from my wallet and tried to jimmy the door latch. Yuck, it was coated with rust, and my card got stuck. Shit! I wrenched the card out and was rewarded with a crumbling sound as the door was freed. With entry gained, I silently crept into the building and felt my way along the back hallway, afraid to turn my flashlight on. The last thing I wanted was to attract attention. The light from a lone street lamp filtering through cobweb encased windows helped guide my path. I half-heard a voice from the front of the complex and inched closer.

"The bitch should be here soon," Andrew was saying. I wasn't sure who he was talking to, but it sure as hell wasn't James.

"No problem," Andrew continued. "I'll get rid of both of them. I owe you after that stint we did in the pen. Mind you, the guy went down easier than I thought, Nigel. Kind of like a fat kid on a teeter-totter." After a pause, he said, "Whoops, sorry, of course I didn't mean to say your name. It's okay, I won't get caught. It's not like anyone is taping this call, and besides, she ain't that smart. Couldn't catch a bagel coming out of a toaster, if ya know what I mean."

So he and Nigel did know each other. Kind of surprising to hear, but no time to think about that now.

Another pause. "So you guys are disappearing?" Andrew asked. "Yeah, I know where to pick up the cash. Once they're dead, I'll just torch the place." Again a pause. Then I heard him say, "Remind me why you and Isadora hired them in the first place." Pause again. "Oh yeah, must have forgot." Another pause, then he said, "I'll meet you on the islands."

I clung to the wall, just outside the office where Andrew's voice was coming from. My heart thumped a paradiddle drumbeat inside my chest. Damn, why hadn't I called the police? Was James already dead? Fat lot of good a can of pepper spray will do me if Andrew has a gun. What was I supposed to do? Throw the can really hard at his head? I grabbed it from my waistband, made sure it was pointed away from me, and peeked around the corner.

Feeble light from a wrought iron ceiling fixture somewhat illuminated the scene. I hadn't a clue why there would still be hydro in this place, but it was a bonus, and I needed to take full advantage. In the scant light and shadows, Andrew sat at a desk with his legs propped and crossed on top. He tossed a gun back and forth between his hands, waiting. His gaze was focused on the front door.

James was slumped on the floor, facing me. His eyes were open, glazed over. I wanted to run to him, make sure he was okay, but in my heart, I knew that wouldn't be a good idea. There were some odd-looking leads with wires attached to his chest. I didn't know a lot about stun guns, but one thing was certain: if James and I were to get out of this alive, I needed to remain calm and in control.

The rise and fall of his chest assured me he was still breathing. Twitching movements from his arms and legs were slight. He was alive! A trickle of blood was already starting to dry on his forehead. Good, there wasn't a lot of it. His gun, from the shooting range, was a few feet away from his hand. I recognized the Glock. No hammer, just fire. I had to get to that gun, but how? There was nothing in my online private investigator course that had prepared me for this!

I had two choices. Plan A was to announce my presence and risk getting shot. Plan B was to create a distraction. Since the pepper spray hadn't been my best friend in the parking lot at the shooting range, I pulled it out and hurled it at the front door of the office.

The clattering noise jolted Andrew from the desk. He jumped up, sending his chair flying. With a gun clenched in his left hand and his back to me, he headed towards the entrance. I waited until the distance was right, then dove to the floor, rolled over, and reached for the Glock. Almost had it, just a fingertip away, when Andrew raced back, tripped over the chair, and fell on top of me.

His sudden weight left me struggling to breathe. I tried to roll him off, but ended up flat on my back. His breath was on my face, his eyes bulged, and a familiar sneer on his lips, in the dim light. "You are one crazy lady. Now you're going down with him," Andrew challenged.

I struggled to find a position. Anything that would allow me to knee him or find an opportunity to escape. He still had the gun in his hand, with the muzzle pointed at my forehead. Otherwise, I'd have tried to poke my thumbs in his eyes. With a slight turn of my head to the left, I saw James's eyes were half open, as if trying to focus. *Buy some time*, James's eyes silently beckoned. At least that was my interpretation of what his eyes were saying.

It was time to try a different tactic. Since Plan A and Plan B hadn't worked, it was time to drop down to Plan C, a.k.a. *connect*.

"Okay, so ya got me. I'm down." I had to think fast. Appeal to Andrew's ego. "Guess you're smarter than me," I said.

I heard movement to my left, ignored it, and focused on the rat in front of me. "Guess it's too late to apologize for the hot tub fiasco. Honestly it wasn't me. I was just following orders," I lied.

Andrew's eyes narrowed. "What do you mean?"

"What can I say? I'm new to the job. Guess we all make mistakes." I paused. "I think James was taking advantage of me, being a newbie investigator and all. Do you have any idea how embarrassing that is? Plus, he didn't even pay me for the job. Do you know how demeaning that is?" I forced some tears to well up in my eyes, just for effect. Given that I was already in pain, it didn't require a whole lot of effort.

Andrew's face was starting to display a hint of confusion, or perhaps he was feeling a kinship with me, for having to work for a boss who gave all the orders.

It was time to press on. "Not sure who you're working for now, but man, you sure did a damn fine job with the church shooting. Plus, you got away with it," I said.

By now Andrew was almost smiling, gloating, and seemed distracted. The gun was still in his hand, no longer pointed at my head.

It was time to load on the gravy. "The cops have been looking for you forever, and they can't find you. You're a pro! Maybe you can give me a few pointers. I sure could use help from a smart guy like you."

I maintained eye contact. Reached towards where I'd last seen the Glock. Felt around on the floor. Finally, the touch of cold metal; I inched it closer and, at last, into the palm of my hand. *No hammer*, I remembered.

Meanwhile, Andrew was spouting off a diatribe about bosses, bad luck, and being underpaid.

I grabbed the gun, aimed it at his head, and pulled the trigger.

Just before I fired, he took hold of my wrist and bent it back. The bullet flew up. Damn! The chain of the suspended ceiling light exploded and dangled in the air. Next thing I knew, the heavy ceiling light was hurtling downward on an angle. Andrew bore the brunt as it crashed into him, landing on his head and back. The light had to have weighed at least twenty pounds. He shrieked in pain. His eyes widened with terror. Mine probably looked like that too.

I managed to push him off as he shouted in pain. Seconds later, he stopped moving. James belly crawled across the floor, pulling the leads from the stun gun off his chest. His voice was slurred, and his movements uncoordinated. He clumsily reached towards his back pocket, extracted a pair of handcuffs, and tossed them in my direction. They skittered across the concrete floor. I clutched them in both hands.

"Cuff 'em," James said.

Holy shit, I'd never put anyone in handcuffs before. Hell, I didn't even know how to use them. Maybe I could figure it out on the fly. It seemed simple enough. I looked at the metal wristbands. Was I supposed to cuff his hands together in the back or in the front? Or should I put one band around his wrist and the other attached to some immovable object?

I put one band around my own wrist, just to test it, so I could figure out how to lock the damn thing. Shit, it snapped shut! Andrew was starting to come to. There was no time to think. I quickly wrapped the other band around his left wrist. Wasn't sure if it was locked or not, but the next thing I knew, there was another *click*. I was trapped to a rat!

James was crawling towards me, now on his hands and knees. His breathing was more even, and he pulled his cell phone out of his pocket. "Geez, Diana, just stay put."

Andrew was getting more active, tossing restlessly and trying to stand up. The last thing I wanted was an angry one-hundred-and-eighty-pound man dragging me across the floor in an escape attempt. I balled my free hand into a fist and aimed a blow at his forehead. It was a solid connect. Sounded like a bat hitting a ball. Satisfaction flooded through me as he went down, like the sack of shit he was, and lay motionless on the floor. This was better than the nose strike to little Mikey Patterson in grade three. Mikey had just been practice; this one hurt a whole lot more. Would I need another cast?

My adrenalin rush was in overdrive. "God, James, are you okay?" I asked.

But his voice was no longer slurred, and he was upright, on his feet, rattling off the address to a 911 dispatcher.

After he hung up, he squatted beside me and took my free hand in his. "Diana, remind me never to piss you off," he said.

It was his next line that assured me he was truly alright.

"That was one helluva shot. Now I know why you were aiming at the ceiling lights in Shooters."

19

With A Little Help from My Friends,
THE BEATLES

First responders were all over the scene, thanks to James's call to 911. I slumped against the wall of the main entrance and tried to stay calm as the cops and ambulance arrived. The paramedics loaded Andrew none too gently onto a stretcher and handcuffed him to the rail. A goose egg-sized lump began to erupt on his forehead, and his shrieks and moans filtered through the rear doors of the ambulance. He wailed like his brains had been caught in his zipper. I loved it. The twerp deserved some pain after what he'd just put me through.

My fist was a bit swollen, but damn it felt good. *He'll blame his head wounds on the ceiling light fixture,* I told myself. No one needed to know that I actually hit him, and I was pretty sure James would turn a blind eye to that.

The entire area was awash with flashing lights, cops, paramedics, even fire trucks. The looky-loos were starting to turn up, and I recognized the news truck that had been dispatched when the

Muff Dive burned down. All were held back by the yellow caution tape that seemed to appear as if by magic. It was a blur, and I didn't even know how much time had passed.

James was only a few feet away, giving a report to the officer on the scene. He kept checking in with me through eye contact, and it was reassuring. Inside the yellow-taped section, it was all procedure: reporting, collecting, organizing information. It was outside that was chaotic. Being an isolated factory area, I couldn't figure out where they were coming from—locals with their cell phones taking pictures, reporters with their microphones and cameras. The din was worse than the sirens.

A uniformed police officer approached me. "You again," he said.

I recognized him from the church fiasco. He was the officer who'd asked some the questions. "Yup, me again." I pasted on my best innocent smile.

"You sure seem to have a knack for finding trouble, ma'am." His tone was suspicious, like he didn't trust me. But hey, this whole thing wasn't my fault.

"Take it easy on the lady," James said. He was immediately at my side, interrupting the officer's flow. "No one talks to her without me present. She just saved my life."

The officer took a step back. The expression on his face went from speculative to respectful in an instant. "Whoa, in that case, let me thank you. You're one brave young woman." The officer stood up straight, before giving me a silent salute. "Thanks for saving one of our own."

"The officer on scene already has my preliminary report, and we'll be heading to the precinct in a few minutes. Give us some space here," James said to the officer.

James waited until the officer left before coming closer; his eyes concerned, questioning. "Are you alright, Diana?"

"Yeah, I'm fine." My hands trembled, my voice sounded shaky, even to me, and I was starting to feel a bit weak in the knees. The adrenalin rush was winding down, and now came the aftermath. Since this was my third rush in as many weeks, I should have been getting used to it by now. This time was the worst. We both could have been killed.

"I don't think you're fine. Come with me," James said. "We'll be out of sight and hearing, at least for a few minutes."

I allowed myself to be led around the corner, back into the alley. Welcomed the comfort of his arms as they wrapped around me, held me close, not letting go. Silent tears trickled down my cheeks, and yuck, my nose was starting to run.

"It's okay, Diana. You did great. If it wasn't for you, I'd be dead."

He pulled away, gently tilted my chin up to meet his gaze—his grey-green eyes intense, filled with gratitude and something else I couldn't quite put my finger on. "You're a great partner, and there's no one I'd trust more to have my back than you, Diana Darling."

That did it. It tore me apart. I burst into a full-out sobbing session. He pulled me closer. It reminded me of the scene from the movie *Speed* with Keanu Reeves and Sandra Bullock where they narrowly escaped death in a subway. Except he'd been on top of her, and I think they actually kissed. Shit, I really needed to get my act together. Besides, I really needed to blow my nose. James didn't seem like the kind of guy to carry a handkerchief or a pack of Kleenex with him, and the last thing I wanted was to have him go home and look at a snot-decorated shirt.

I took a quivering inhale before placing my hands on his chest, giving him a slight push. "Give me a minute to collect myself. I'll see you around the corner," I said.

"Are you sure?"

"Yes, go now." *Before I change my mind*, I thought.

Wow, James considered me a partner. His touch had left me more weak-kneed than the downside of the adrenalin rush. I glanced at the long sleeves of my Wally Mart blouse. Unbuttoned the cuff, did a huge soggy nasal blow, and rolled it up past my elbow. Thank God for wash-and-wear clothes. It was time to get back on track.

I glanced up. True to form, there was Mom. Well, actually it was a cloud passing over the moon, but it looked like there was a smile on it. At any rate, I knew it was her. Mom never ever let me down, even if it was just my imagination.

I pulled myself together and rounded the corner at full tilt. James was waiting, and I almost knocked him over. "Andrew and Nigel knew each other," I burst out. "I overheard Andrew's conversation in the office. It sounds like they did some time together in the pen. We have a new lead here, James."

"That's my partner," he said. "Always on the job."

Still he gave me another concerned look. I brushed it off. "What's next?" I asked.

"From here, we'll go to the station. There'll be lots of questions. Be honest with your answers, and I'll be right there with you."

The very thought of getting into my car and driving seemed beyond me. James was already being summoned back by the investigator on the scene.

James must have read my mind because he said, "Officer, take this lady to the station and make sure she's well-looked-after. Diana, I'm just going to finish up here, and I'll meet you in about twenty minutes."

I nodded, followed the officer to the police car, crawled into the back seat, and took note of the missing door handles and the wire mesh that separated me from the driver. It was another first for me. Well, almost a first. The last time I'd been in the back of a cruiser wasn't really my fault, and my memories of it were faint. I blame it on my so-called friend Dorothy Calhoun. Hell, she had a villainous name, and I should have known better. She was only a couple of years older than me, and I'd followed her lead. We had smoked a bit of pot and gotten a sudden case of the munchies.

She'd goaded me into stealing a jar of peanut butter from the local grocery store. The store manager had not been impressed, caught me with my finger in the container, and called the cops. For most of that ride to the station, I was stoned and trying to lick the damn peanut butter that was stuck to the roof of my mouth. Fortunately, Mom bailed me out, there were no charges, and the last I'd heard of Dorothy Calhoun, she was doing prison time for grand theft auto, after breaking through the window of a doublewide, at a trailer park in Florida, to steal the keys.

This time, however, I was being treated like royalty. The officer escorted me from the car into the station.

"What can I get you to drink?" the officer asked. I'd have killed for a double martini, didn't need it to be shaken, only slightly jiggled, but settled for a bottle of water instead. There was a comfortable chair to sit in while I waited. I was still trying to figure out how James had been caught by Andrew. James was an ex-cop, smart, and excellent with a pistol. How in hell had Andrew managed to nail him with a stun gun?

The station was abuzz, and I noticed a lot of the officers giving me sidelong glances of appreciation. *Once a cop, always a cop*, I figured. They protect their own. It was a far cry from working for the government where everyone seemed suspicious, and everything had to be done in duplicate. There were checkers, and then there were people who checked the checkers. Talk about bureaucracy. Sure we'd track down bad guys, or people who tried to rip off the system, but I'd never seen someone with a gun. They were white-collar criminals instead. Note to self: most of the perps in the police station seem to be handcuffed in the back.

The front doors of the station swished open, and there was James. His stride was confident; his face a mask of professionalism. I felt my internal engine turn over and hum, but the timing was all off. It wasn't the right time, and it sure wasn't the right place. I wondered if it ever would be.

James approached, and once again I saw the concern beneath his mask. I jumped up—my way of letting him know I was okay—but damn, my sleeve was stuck to the arm of the chair. I wrestled it free and tried to hide my other hand that was now swollen and bruised.

He glanced at the officer with him. "Ice bag, now, then we'll get her statement."

In minutes, I was in a barren interview room, just a table, three chairs, and a two-way mirror. I rested the cold gel pack on the back of my hand and welcomed the instant pain relief.

"Diana, this is Detective Reagan. He and I were partners a few years back. I've already filled him in on some of the details. He still needs to interview you before I can take you home."

"Sure, go ahead." I said, wondering which *home* James was referring to. Really hoped I'd be spending the night at his condo instead of my single bed in the storage room. But of course, there was Xena to consider. Not fair to my kitty, and I wasn't sure James would welcome her at his place.

Reagan wasn't at all like James. He had a fatherly look about him with soft eyes, even though they'd probably seen too much. His suit was off-the-rack, his shirt wrinkled, and his tie askew. It made me feel comfortable.

"Could you start from the beginning? Help me understand how you came to be at the warehouse?" Reagan asked.

"No problem." I launched into a litany that included the phone call from Andrew, my knowledge of the building layout, and how I knew to sneak in through the back door.

Reagan nodded and took notes. "What about the phone call you overheard? Tell me about that."

This guy was good. No leading questions, even though he already knew Andrew had been on the phone with Nigel. I was sure James told Reagan all about that phone call.

I recited verbatim what I'd overheard. James's eyes locked with mine; he gave a slight nod before I continued. As I spoke, I left out the emotional stuff I felt, trying to keep it strictly to the facts. But when it came time to explain the gunshot to the ceiling light, I did have to embellish a bit. "Once he grabbed my wrist, there was nowhere else to aim but up. The light looked heavy. It was a lucky shot," I said.

James's cheek was tweaking and Reagan stifled a smile. "What about the injury to your hand?" he asked.

"It must have happened when I struggled with Andrew to get the handcuffs on."

"Good enough. I'll be back in a few minutes." As Reagan left the room, he winked at James. I pretended not to notice.

The two-way mirror was obvious. It may as well have had a sign posted that said, "We're watching you." Since it wasn't actually an interrogation, I presumed no one was behind it. Besides, I couldn't wait any longer.

"James, for God's sake, how on earth did you ever let that guy nail you with a stun gun?"

He winced, looking down. Holy crap, was James having a weak moment?

"I found Andrew at the convenience store where he'd last used his credit card. He told me he was holding you hostage. It was a no-brainer. No time to call the cops. I had to find you," James said.

I smiled. Maybe James wasn't the bulletproof kind of guy he presented himself as, most of the time. I knew somewhere deep down there was a soft side. Had I just found it?

20

Slip Slidin' Away,
SIMON AND GARFUNKEL

Three hours later, I was back at James's condo. The view hadn't changed much since the last time, unless you included the total degree of respect with which he now looked at me.

"You saved my life today, Diana."

"I know." My inner voice was shrieking, my thoughts were all over the map, but I had to figure out what would keep him intrigued. I needed to do that because I wanted to keep him in my life. Best case scenario for me, go back to talking about the case. That way, James had to stick around.

"So what happens next with Andrew?" I asked.

"He'll be charged, probably attempted murder, assault, and whatever else the prosecutor can drum up. Plus if the ladies he bamboozled at the couples retreat wanted to get together on a class-action lawsuit, he could wind up owing a pile of cash, on top of being behind bars for an extra long time."

"What about his connection with Nigel?" I swivelled on the bar stool at his bar-style kitchen island and tried to ignore my tummy rumblings. Wasn't sure if it was hunger or perhaps a post-adrenalin let-down after the trauma I'd just been through. He must have caught my glance at the refrigerator. Minutes later, there was a platter of three kinds of cheese, seedless green grapes separated into tiny bunches, and four types of crackers. I munched. He talked.

"Definitely a follow-up related to Nigel is required, thanks to you." He paused. "You never did tell me where you got the information on him."

I debated telling James the truth. What would he think if he knew I hired Bambi to be my receptionist? I'd just saved his life. That should count for some kind of forgiveness, shouldn't it? I swallowed a chunk of Edam cheese on a rice cracker and said, "Well, to be honest, I have a new receptionist, and she's really good at sussing things out."

"Business must be going well for you then. That's great."

Perfect timing. His phone rang, and I welcomed the reprieve as he headed to the window, away from me. In the meantime, I snatched more cheese and crackers and wiped crumbs from my lips before he returned.

His face looked excited; his body animated. What was that all about?

He rested his elbows on the island across from me, looked directly in my eyes, and I was lost for an instant.

"Diana, I know it's been a really long day. Have to ask though. Are you up for one more adventure? Not tonight, but it will need to be really early in the morning."

Hell yes, I was thinking. *Anything to spend more time with . . .* "Absolutely," I replied.

"That was a buddy of mine from the police force. They have an address for Isadora LaPorte, and we need to check out her place."

"What if she's home?" I asked.

"She ain't home, and garbage pickup is tomorrow. We need to get there before the garbage trucks do. I'll drive you back to your office now. Just be prepared. There might be some dumpster diving involved. You okay with a 6:00 a.m. start?"

I nodded. I'd never been up that early in my life—well, maybe once, or even twice. Escaping before dawn was a prerequisite when you'd spent the night with a guy whose first name you couldn't remember. Damn, shades of my misspent youth. At least this time, I didn't have to sneak out. The only requirement was remembering to set the alarm clock and trying to figure out what the heck to wear for diving into a dumpster! Would I need a ladder, or would a foot stool suffice? How tall were those things anyway? Perhaps James could just give me a leg up, even though I would have preferred it be a leg *over* in a different setting.

...

At 6:10 a.m., we were on a mission. The address was 2350 Haviture Way, in a middle- to high-income residential area just north of the main town. James drove, and I rode shotgun. No real guns this time, and that was just fine with me. I smelled enough cordite and heard enough gunshots in the last few days to last me a lifetime. My hand still hurt, but thanks to the ice bag I slept with, the swelling had gone down, and I'd been rewarded with semi-full dexterity.

For this job, all I required was a pair of rubber gloves from the dollar store, some castoff fishing boots from my dad and a pair of sweatpants and a shirt courtesy of Goodwill. It annoyed me a little that James wouldn't be adding to my wardrobe. Besides, one never knew when a hazmat suit might become the new fashion craze. Since I already had the Choos, the Hermès bag, and the little black dress from Paris, I figured I could handle this. No addition to my wardrobe required.

I'd never been dumpster diving before, so I really wasn't sure what to expect.

"So, James, what is it we're looking for here?" I asked.

He eased his Jeep to a stop near the driveway of Isadora LaPorte's three-story home. The house was all dark, with no car in the driveway and an overflowing mailbox. She obviously hadn't been home for a while, and that explained the full voice mail, as well as the non-response to my e-mails.

"Trust me, Diana. We'll know it when we see it. Ya never know what people throw out in the garbage, and apparently Isadora's been missing for almost a week now. And so has Nigel. It's definitely not a coincidence. Anyways, trash pickup's in a couple of hours, so we need to finish the search before the trucks roll in."

Holy crap, what would people find if they sifted through my stuff? I'd better stash my old *Playgirl* magazines, my dildo vibrator with the elephant tusks, and other unmentionable stuff, like my high school diary, in someone else's bin, just in case. Well, maybe I'd keep the elephant guy. The fact that he used too many batteries wasn't exactly his fault. Perhaps he could be hidden above one of the false ceiling tiles in the bathroom—still available if, and when, I needed him.

I followed the bobbing of James's flashlight just inside the gateway. No lights on inside the somewhat stately mansion that didn't seem like the right fit for Harold. It made me wonder how Isadora had hooked up with him in the first place. I made a mental note to quiz Bambi on this one. Or maybe I could just persuade her to let me interview him directly.

The pathway had some of those solar lights strategically placed, and James was already approaching the target.

"Isn't this trespassing?" I asked.

"Well, technically yes, so hang on a second." He rolled the bins out to the curb. "Better?" he asked. "Now they're on public property, and you're not breaking any laws."

There were two large bins. One for recycling and one for waste. Oh goody, at least they weren't those big metal monstrosities I'd have to crawl into.

"Toss ya for it," James said. Didn't matter if it was heads or tails; with my luck, I'd be getting the wet-waste bin. The coin flipped in the air and landed on the back of his hand.

"Tails. Waste is for you, Diana," he said. It never occurred to me to check the coin. Instead, I followed obediently along.

I pinched my nose in preparation and upended the bin. I gagged and stifled my urge to hurl. Hell, I really should have insisted on being provided a hazmat suit for this job. Gooey, slimy leftover food spilled on the walkway. A couple of empty bottles floated on the ooze of garbage. It was apparent that Isadora wasn't exactly compliant when it came to recycling glass. It was also apparent that Isadora's taste in wine was definitely a couple of notches up compared to mine. Her bottles bore French labels, like Chardonnay and Pinot Grigio. Mine came in a cardboard box with the marking, Dry White.

James was sorting through a bunch of paper in the recycling bin. "Shit," he muttered. "Most of it is shredded. At least it's not from a cross cutter, just a straight cutter."

I hadn't a clue what he was talking about and was about to ask, when my dad's oversized boots made me slip and land ass first in the midst of food leftovers. I reached down and grabbed a large soft meatball thing that had some congealed pasta-like strings attached. At least, that's what I thought it was. I gave the strings a tug to get them out of my way, but they were stuck. I pulled harder, and next thing I knew, they somehow flew up and managed to get their tendrils wrapped around my neck. The strings were thicker at one end, and as for the meatball, it had eyes. Dull, glossed over, and thankfully dead. I was face to face with leftover bits from what appeared to be a jellyfish that had been cooked whole. My right glove flew off as I hurled the offending creature over my shoulder.

I'd eaten jellyfish legs once before at a Chinese restaurant that touted themselves as being authentic. Trust me, those legs looked and tasted like rubber bands. Never seen it cooked with the head still on though.

"Find something?" James asked.

"Nothing worth keeping," I said.

I slipped and slithered in the remaining mess, trying to find my footing. That's when I discovered two books. Why would there be books in the wet waste?

"James, give me some more light here."

His halogen flashlight focused in as I scraped dried remnants from the first cover. The book was entitled *How to Disappear*. The second was a high school yearbook from twenty years ago. Why on earth would anyone trash that?

"Bingo," he said. "That along with the stuff in the recycling bin might give us a clue. Are you any good at puzzles, Diana Darling?"

Puzzles, hell yes. I'd grown up with crossword books and recently completed two Nancy Drew computer games. Even got a high score and assured status of *super sleuth*. "Sure, James, I'm a master at puzzles."

"Good. We'll spend a few more minutes here, go back to my place, and lay everything out." He was already tossing shredded paper into a clear garbage bag and put the books on top.

I kicked a few more offending bits of rubbish from my path and pulled myself up to a standing position. "Shouldn't we be cleaning up here?"

"I understand there's a raccoon infestation in the neighbourhood. Those suckers can open up anything," James said, winking.

I smiled, more than happy to follow him to the Jeep and get the hell away from the garbage.

We were only a few minutes into the drive to his place when he hit the button to crack the window open. "Diana, I reckon you might want to think about showering, or maybe changing your perfume?"

He was right. My sweatpants were soaked in only God knew what. My shirt was caked with dirt, a couple of used dryer sheets clung to my chest, and as I ran my fingers through my hair, a rubber band appeared. Showering was a necessity, but in the meantime, it was time to come clean, figuratively speaking. I'd been holding too much back from him, and the guilt was almost worse than the smell of my clothes.

"Roll the window down a bit lower. You may need it," I said.

"Huh?"

"The extra air, you may need it after what I'm about to tell you."

I was glad it was dark, except for the light from the dashboard. That last thing I wanted to see was the expression on his face, but after the last few days, it was time to get everything out into the open. My big confession didn't take long. In fact, it was easier than fessing up to Mom when I got into trouble as a teen, like that whole pot smoking incident. Mom had actually whacked me, but this was different.

James's silence left me wishing the leather seat would swallow me whole. "So let me get this right," he finally said. "You hired Bambi to be your receptionist? And you have a copy of Nigel's hard drive?"

"That'd be pretty much it." I stared straight ahead. "That's how I got some of the info I gave you in the parking lot at the shooting range."

More silence. Street lamps reflected on the windshield. James grounded the gears as he neared a stop sign. I'd ridden with James other times, and he never grounded the gears before.

"I know there's more on the memory stick, but it's password-protected. Even Bambi couldn't figure it out," I blurted out.

He rested his head on the steering wheel. His hands clenched and unclenched the grip cover. It seemed to take forever, before finally he lifted his head and said, "Diana, you never cease to amaze me. I'm not sure that hiring Bambi was a great idea, but the hard drive we'll need." He easily shifted into first gear, changed lanes, and took the exit towards my office. "Oh, and you're welcome to bring the cat. It could be a long day."

"Thanks James," I said.

At least I didn't have to explain why I hired Bambi. Still I was questioning why Xena had been invited. After all, I left her for a whole two nights to attend the couples retreat, and there was no problem. Was James becoming a sucker for my feline? I was mentally packing a cat carrier, some cat litter, and a disposable container of cat food and treats. Sometimes packing for a cat for an extended trip was like packing for a child. My stuff would fit in a knapsack. Xena needed a house of her own.

As we entered my office, it was only 9:00 a.m. I found a note from Bambi on my desk. Must have missed it yesterday.

It read: "Call me. Got Teddy's kid's snot after he tossed a Kleenex into a bin outside of school. Have sent it off to a private lab for DNA testing. Teddy likes you by the way. Oh, and I'm checking out the insurance company for Dave. As for Deborah, I'm searching social media. Have had a few hits. And by the way, there was another call from that crazy lady, Nikki."

I hid the note from James and pretended to check my phone for messages. There wouldn't be any messages, nevertheless it would buy me some time to recover from finding out that Teddy likes me. Nothing like a little flattery to boost a girl's ego. I found the memory stick, with a copy of Nigel's hard drive, and stuck it in my purse. A three-minute shower later, it was time to pack up and get back to James. He'd be getting impatient.

But I needn't have worried. As I turned towards the hallway, there was James carrying a bag of cat litter. Xena was draped around his neck, looking glad that he was back. Damn fickle cat. "Always gotta have it your way," I muttered. Then I remembered the street we'd just been at: Haviture Way. Mmm, coincidences seemed to be everywhere. Mom was at it again!

21

Jig-Saw Puzzle,
THE ROLLING STONES

Back at James's place, I was definitely in charge of the puzzles. It appeared I'd graduated from wet waste to recycling. Now I understood the difference between shredders. Much to my surprise, it was really interesting, and it probably helped to be a tad OCD. Cross cutters chopped everything into confetti-sized pieces, and there was no way the paper could be reconstructed. Straight cutters just sliced everything into strips, and that was a bonus for me. The only problem was there was one hell of a huge bag full of the stuff. I looked for colours first and sorted them into piles. There's a big difference between white, off-white, and beige. Then, I looked for textures of paper—yup, more mini piles. James's condo was starting to resemble a paper factory that had just been blown up.

I didn't care. I would milk this until the cows came home, just to be there with James. I was so engrossed in my work that I almost missed out on all the fun he was having with Xena. James had shown her the litter box, poured a splash of milk into a bowl, and they were sucking up to each other to no end.

"Hello," I shouted. "Isn't anyone going to help me here?"

"Sorry, Diana. Sounds like you're hungry."

Damn, he knew me well. "Well, I could be tempted to eat something, just as long as it doesn't have legs that look like tentacles."

James gave me a quizzical look. "Well, it's too early in the morning for seafood. How about some Eggs Benedict on whole-wheat toast? I'll give Xena some tuna and pour the water over her dried food." She was wrapped around his arm, giving him her most soulful gaze. *Damn*, I thought. If I really wanted to lure James, I should be taking lessons from my cat!

...

Two hours later, I managed to put some of the strips of paper together, stuck them on a poster board, and they were meshing into place. A document that looked like it was for a bank account in the Cayman Islands, a receipt for two plane tickets purchased five days ago (destination still lost in the paper pile), and a receipt for Chinese takeout, including a jellyfish side dish. The dinner was courtesy of a popular chain restaurant that delivered. Since most of the jellyfish had been found in the bin, I reckoned it hadn't been a hit.

Nigel's signature was scrawled across the bottom for the plane ticket receipt in huge, indecipherable letters, written straight up and with an underscore. Handwriting analysis had been one of my mother's specialties, so I learned from her that if your writing has a backward slant, it means you have a lot of unresolved conflicts and dwell on them; if your writing has a forward slant, it indicates you are future-minded. Nigel's signature indicates someone who has a super-inflated ego, is self-absorbed, and considers himself God's gift to women, thus the flourished underscore with an upward swing under his name.

Back to the situation at hand, there was no doubt in my mind, I'd been set up. We both had. Our clients knew each other, and for the life of me, I couldn't come up with any solid reasoning behind it. Were we a distraction for something bigger? And where Andrew came into the picture, I hadn't a clue.

"What do you think, James? Should we take a look at that high school yearbook? There has to be some reason it was thrown out recently."

The memory stick was shoved into the side of his laptop, and he was busy pressing keys. "Sounds good, I haven't yielded much here," he said, slamming down the lid of his laptop and heading to the table where the books were.

I used a damp sponge to clean the leather cover. Mind you, it did nothing to help the pages from sticking together. Once a few of the pages were peeled apart, we flipped to the graduating class—it was from one of the local high schools, albeit a few decades back. The pictures were in black and white, with the tallest students standing in the back row. The second row was mostly the same. And then in the front row, students were seated.

Wow, the girls' teased hairdos complete with streaks courtesy of peroxide, short skirts, and fishnet stockings were a sign of the times. Some guys wore ties; others just got away with T-shirts and jeans. I really wasn't sure what we were looking for until James read the names under the photo. Holy crap, there was Nigel on the far left. Isadora was front and centre with knee-socks and running shoes. Next, was the kicker! Andrew was in the back row on the right.

"Holy shit," I said. "They all know each other."

"You're right. We've been purposely led off the trail. Probably hired us to lead the police to Bambi and Harold where most of the emphasis would have been, given they're having an affair. Since both Isadora and Nigel are now missing, some people may even presume they're dead. Their spouses would be the most logical suspects."

"Damn slimeballs," I muttered. "Gives me a whole new reason to check out the other book, *How to Disappear*."

"Go for it," he said. "See if they dog-eared any particular pages."

His cell phone vibrated on the kitchen counter. Xena leapt up, spun the phone around, then gave it a swat, and James managed to catch it just before it hit the floor.

I was still admiring the speed of his reflexes, along with the chiselled outline of his butt under his jeans, when I heard, "What the fuck?" He motioned me to turn the TV on to the news channel.

"The charred remains of two bodies have just been recovered from the trunk of a car in a ravine north of town," the reporter was saying. "Police are on the scene. Initial reports indicate it may be difficult to determine the identities, given the destruction to the vehicle. We'll have more on this breaking news at noon. The weather is next."

I struggled to contain myself. Couldn't wait for James to get off the phone. That area of town was familiar to me, since that's where I had my first horizontal date in the back seat of a car. It had been instigated by a bottle of lemon gin. *Panty remover*, they called it back then, with a pimply faced guy, whose name I didn't recall in the haze of the aftermath. I recalled the location as being more of a deep ditch than a ravine, but then again, gravity takes its toll. The plot was definitely getting thicker, and I couldn't wait to hear what came next.

James was still on the phone, nodding. "Great stuff. I owe you big time, Reagan. Sure, I'll keep you posted from my end."

After hanging up, his smile was teasing, and he was holding back, until I reminded him, "Hey, didn't I just save your life?"

"True, but you never told me about Bambi. Guess we're even."

I agreed, though I wasn't sure saving lives equated to hiring practices.

"Andrew's lawyered up, but he did admit he was hired by Nigel. The licence plate of the car in the ravine has been traced to Isadora. Same make and model. The bodies are burned beyond recognition. Even with DNA testing, it will take forever to determine exact identities," James said.

"James, what if it's really them and they are dead?"

"Trust me, Diana. It's more likely they're trying to delay any pursuit."

"Shouldn't we be checking out the scene?" Part of me wanted him to say *yes*. Not sure why I wanted to see a couple of burned up bodies, but perhaps I could chalk it up to a learning experience. My hopes were soon dashed.

"Nah, Reagan will feed me whatever info he has. That leaves us with the memory stick. The earlier stuff you gave me is great, but there has to be a lot more here." He was busy pouring over his computer. "Just need a password for files marked Top Secret. Stupid name for a file," he mumbled. "Now when it comes to password protection, most times people aren't exactly too creative."

"Try his date of birth."

"Been there, done that already."

There was nothing I learned in my course that would help me here, however I knew from personal experience, passwords needed to have eight characters and preferably include a number or something else to make them unique.

"What about *Password 1!* With an exclamation mark?"

"Why that one?" he asked.

"Because when I forgot my password once, that's what they sent me."

He grimaced after trying it out. "Nope, that's not working either."

"What about his street address and adding an exclamation mark at the end?" I was grasping at straws. But seconds later, James erupted.

"We're in."

I looked over his shoulder and inhaled the scent of Old Spice. Holy shit! There were e-mails back and forth between Isadora and Nigel. Some of them were definitely not on the business side of things.

"Can't wait to see you again. Next time let's go for the mask and tickle feather. I'm dying to tease you."

"Hold onto that thought. Soon we'll be together, and you can tease me all night. Not long now. The island awaits us. Sweetie Pie, do you think they'll find the handcuffs in my luggage?"

"Don't think so. They're made of elastic and Velcro, not metal." The message was followed by a couple of those smiley face icons.

There was a lot more, but I'd had enough of the kinky stuff. I left James to read through the messages and headed to the book, *How to Disappear*. It covered everything from leaving false trails to vanishing without a trace. There was something about erasing your digital footprint, but since my feet have toes, I really wasn't sure what that meant. Some of the sections were marked with a yellow highlighter, including "not using your credit card." That was a no-brainer, wasn't it? I presumed they must have missed the last chapter entitled, "Don't leave anything in your trash."

So back to the shredded piles of paper I went. Thirty minutes later, just when I had everything reasonably organized, Xena took a tear through and romped across my carefully sorted piles. Shit, I'd have to start over. As much as I loved my cat, now was looking like a really good time to rehome her.

James must have caught my look. "No worries, Diana," he said. "From what I gather here, they faked their deaths and are headed to the Cayman Islands. Offshore bank account included." That matched up with what I'd found on the strips of paper.

"All the upfront stuff of hiring you and me, along with Andrew's actions, was just to throw everyone off the case. Do you know anything about offshore banking?" James asked.

"Well, I used to be a number cruncher for a government revenue agency. Basic information, I can provide," I said. He didn't seem the least bit surprised. Hell, he probably knew that about me already, so I decided to give him the Coles Notes 101 version on banking outside of the US. "First of all there's greater privacy, little or no taxation, and easy access to deposits."

"Mmm, makes sense. What else?" he asked.

"It's often associated with organized crime via tax evasion and money laundering."

"Okay, I don't peg them as the mob type. But the tax evasion and escaping sounds more probable."

He rested his chin on his hands, as if pondering. Xena gave him a nudge, which he seemed to ignore. Crap, he really must have been thinking hard to not have responded to Xena.

She eventually settled in my lap. I took it as a sign. "So, James. What's next?"

He stood up; his facial demeanour indicating a plan was in place. "Do you have an up-to-date passport?"

I grinned. "As long as I don't have to show you my picture, I'm good."

"Huh," he said, "I'll show you mine, if you show me yours." James winked.

When I didn't respond, he said, "I'll have Melanie call you with flight details. Looks like we're heading to the Cayman Islands, and we'll try departing tomorrow."

"Sounds good." Already I was thinking about what to pack and how to find a sitter for my cat since I wasn't sure how long we'd be gone.

"I'm heading to my office. I'll arrange for a car to take you and Xena home. You may as well leave all the cat accoutrements here. She seems to like my place. Besides, you both may need to visit again before this case is over."

One hour later, I returned home to find Bambi pouring over a binder at the reception desk. Oh, oh, it was the manual from my online PI course!

22

Oh, Pretty Woman,
ROY ORBISON

Bambi raised her eyebrows and gave me an all-knowing stare. One that was reminiscent of how Mom used to look at me when I'd been caught colouring outside the lines, or otherwise misbehaving.

Xena jumped from my arms and raced to the desk to sit on the file folders beside Bambi. I kept silent. Crap, now she knew the truth about me.

"So," Bambi finally said. "I'm already up to chapter three, and so far, it's been pretty entertaining. I will, however, be requiring a raise."

Huh, since I wasn't actually paying her, aside from a percentage on business she brought in, I wondered what was going on. She continued, "I'm already getting a 93% in the online course, and that's with no do-overs. Found your username and password inside the manual. Hope you don't mind I've been using it. Plus, I've picked up another new client. Some guy who says you helped him out at a hockey arena has referred his brother."

I waited. For yet another time in my life, silence seemed to be the best response, even though I consistently broke that rule.

"I'll be taking 33% per cent of any business I bring in," Bambi said.

Since I hadn't really stated a number before, I reckoned it was time to negotiate. "How about 25%?"

"Not happening. I've already given you a copy of Nigel's hard drive and brought Teddy, Deborah, and Dave your way. You owe me."

Her voice sounded firm. No room for flexibility. Plus, I knew I'd be looking for an immediate cat sitter, and perhaps that could equate to the extra 8% she was demanding.

"It's a deal," I said. "But, I'm going to need more help here."

"Like how?"

I walked her through the last twenty-four hours. Explained the whole situation with James, the dumpster diving, the yearbook, the bodies in the car, what we found out from the hard drive, and how I'd be heading to the Cayman Islands tomorrow.

The first words out of her mouth confirmed I'd made a good decision in hiring her. "I'll look after Xena. Don't you worry."

As I breathed a sigh of relief, she interjected, "Too bad about your wardrobe."

"Huh?"

"I've checked out your closet, or rather the place where most normal people would store brooms. Your clothes totally suck, except for a really nice expensive pair of high-heeled shoes and an awesome black dress, neither of which are really appropriate for an island visit. Let me take you shopping."

I hesitated for two good reasons. First, I didn't exactly have a lot of cash to spend on clothes, and second, her taste didn't really match mine. I've seen her squeezed into those tube tops and spandex pants. Mind you, when I looked at her today, she seemed totally presentable. Black pressed pants, low high-heeled boots, and a tangerine zippered jacket.

"Don't worry about money. My sister owns a place called the Clothes Barn. They buy clothes from estate sales and from stores going out of business. It's sold by the pound. But don't you worry, you'll get the friends and family discount, a.k.a. it's free!" Bambi said.

The last word was like music to my ears, and I could hardly wait!

...

The Clothes Barn lived up to its name. A two-story boarded building that looked like it belonged on a farm. I wondered about the estate stuff. Did that mean I'd be getting clothes from a deceased person? I'd rather wear whatever came from the stores going out of business. How in hell was I supposed to be able to tell the difference?

Bambi heaved one of the wooden double doors open, and I followed. Holy crap! Instead of clothes being organized by style, like pants on one rack, blouses on another, skirts in another section, these clothes were organized by colour. Some were dumped in big white plastic laundry bins you had to sort through. Some were actually hung on racks, while others dangled from ceiling hangers that would require a stepladder to reach. On the left side of the place, everything was white. Moving across to the middle, it went from yellow to orange, red, purple, and blue. The second floor was reserved for grey and black clothes, according to the sign that read, "Formal or Funeral Wear."

We were immediately greeted by a saleslady, who I soon gathered was Bambi's sister. "Bambi, great to see you here. You've brought a customer. Tell me, what does she need? Don't tell me she's from the Muff Dive. You know we sell stuff by the pound. I sure can't make a living off someone like her!"

Bambi's sister looked as if she were in her fifties, with dyed red hair and eyeglasses that dangled from a chain. Her blue denim shirt had a name tag that read, *Monita*. Oh My God, that was my mother's name, even though she'd insisted on being called Marie. I felt like I'd been dropped into an episode of the *Twilight Zone*, but I'd missed the beginning. Part of me wanted to say, "Mom, I can look after myself." On the other hand, it was comforting to know she was there with me in spirit.

"Nah," said Bambi. "She's not a stripper, even though I keep telling her she has the body for it. This is Diana, a friend of mine, and she's heading to the Cayman Islands tomorrow. What have you got that's tropical?"

"Go for the middle section." Monita pointed at the coloured bins and hangers. "Have at it. Next time bring a paying customer though, will ya?"

...

Two hours later, we amassed three garbage bags full of clothes. Since there weren't any change rooms, and no mirrors, I had to guess on the sizing. Some stuff I tried on over my clothes to check if it fit. A lot of the clothes looked new, and there were still some articles that had old, yellowed price tags on them. Hopefully I wasn't getting any of the estate goods.

We were on our way home when I had to ask, "How come your sister doesn't just put price tags on the clothes?"

"Trust me. Her turnover is so high and fast, she'd have to hire someone to do that, and it would cut down on her profits.

It's easier and cheaper to go by weight, plus her deals are usually cash only."

It made sense to me, in some kind of fashion. Besides, this whole shopping escapade had been free, and the price was right. Way better than Wally Mart. Back at the office, I sorted through my new purchases, or acquired items rather, then packed my bag, and kissed Xena, even though she turned her nose up at me and willingly followed Bambi out of the office to spend the next few days at the Whispering Pines motel. The light on my phone was blinking—a phone message from Melanie indicating the details for tomorrow's flight. Wonderful, it was leaving at 6:10 a.m.

23

Come Fly with Me,
FRANK SINATRA

There were two things I hated about flying. Number one was being trapped in a winged metal tube loaded with ignitable fluids, piloted by someone I didn't know. Not reassuring. Number two was something I learned from my first ex-husband, who was an air traffic controller. He was kind of like a traffic cop at a three-dimensional intersection. I'd never forget the nights he came home, with his hair standing on end and eyes bugging out, telling me about *near misses*. I shuddered. But since driving to an island was out of the question, and a boat would take too long, I'd have to take my chances in the air.

So here I was with James, on a 747 headed for the Cayman Islands, to track down Isadora and Nigel. "You okay with flying?" James asked. "You look a little nervous."

"Yup, I'm good with short hauls, but otherwise my arms get tired."

He shook his head. "That's a really old joke. Still, you've got one wicked sense of humour. I love that about you."

Did he just mention the word *love*? Love doesn't usually make me feel sick, but my heart knocked against my chest with an increased beat, and my stomach started to churn. Flying and emotions were a strong mix, and I wanted to be ready. When he wasn't looking, I downed a couple of Gravol Quick Dissolve tablets and located the airsick bag, just in case.

We were in something called *plus class*, a step up from economy, so James had a little more legroom. His six-foot frame still left his knees close to the seatback ahead. If he folded the table down, it would very likely be on a slant. I watched as the flight attendants walked the aisles, ensuring everything was stowed away in overhead bins before takeoff. There was one little wannabe hotty who kept coming back to check on James. Her collagen-inflated lips looked painful, and I wondered about the rest of her plastic face. The dead giveaway was the turkey wattle wobbling at the underside of her neck. There was also her underarm jiggle as she hefted a light bag into the overhead bin. If she was less than sixty, I'd be surprised.

"Let me know if there's anything you need." Her emphasis on *anything* and her come-on smile were easily translated. Yikes, it was also the same line Teddy had used on me at the Muff Dive. I must have been missing a whole new dictionary of clichéd pick-up lines.

I fastened my seatbelt before the attendants had a chance to demonstrate it. You'd have to be really stupid not to figure that one out since seatbelts in cars had been required for years. Then, I also located the exit doors, just in case an escape was required. The flight personnel did the requisite finger pointing to demonstrate the use of oxygen masks and, God forbid, the inflatable life vests since we were flying over water. Yes, I knew how to blow into a tube, even though the last time was related to a sobriety test when I got pulled over after leaving a wine bar. I'd managed to dodge that bullet. Apparently the officer who pulled me over was a customer of my mother's and recognized the address on my driver's licence. I made sure she gave him a discount on his next visit!

Next, I checked out the other passengers on the plane. Oh joy, we were in the middle of kiddy central. Across the aisle, a screaming toddler slapped his mother. She told him he was a good boy.

In the seat ahead, a young girl, about age six, poked her head over and shouted, "I feel like I'm gonna puke."

I tossed her the little barf bag from my seat pocket and gave her the look my mother used to give me when I misbehaved. One eyebrow raised and a stern smile that read, *I dare you*. "Not on me. Use this instead," I said.

Her eyes widened, her mouth dropped, and she disappeared. *Good*, I thought. Reckon that'd be the last we saw of her on this ride.

I flexed my muscles, tried to control the churning in my gut, and asked James, "How long is this flight again?"

"Should be about three hours. In the meantime, catch up on some rest. We'll go over the itinerary once we land and get checked into the hotel."

We could do it now, I was thinking. Then, I remembered we were in close quarters, and everyone else could overhear. Not a good idea. James was right. I settled back into my seat as the plane rolled onto the runway. Engines whined, wheels rumbled and jerked on the tarmac; the aircraft picked up speed, a final jerk, and then lift off. We were in the air. The absence of the little barf bag taunted me from the seat pocket in front. Damn, how long did it take for those anti-nausea pills to work, and why didn't I remember to take them earlier?

Twenty minutes later, the plane levelled off. I was feeling better and unclenched my hands from the armrests. Great, the Lip Lady was back. "Can I get you a beverage? Something from the bar?" she asked.

Her attention was directed towards James, but when he clasped my hand and said, "I think we're fine here," she disappeared. The expression on her face was priceless. *Hunt somewhere else*, I was thinking. If the Muff Dive hadn't burned down, I'd be giving her the address. She'd be a perfect second fiddle to Tribal Tits.

"Thanks for rescuing me," James said.

"Mmm, that seems to be a habit of mine."

He winked. I smiled.

James passed a few brochures my way. "So this is where we'll be staying. The hotel has an ocean view, and it's close to the banking district. I've pulled in a few favours that I'll explain later."

The Gravol was starting to take hold, and I leaned my head against the window, while sorting through the flyers. Knew I would be drifting soon and hoped I wouldn't snore. I closed my eyes and thought about the new wardrobe that was waiting to be displayed. Also thought about seeing James in tight swim trunks and a tropical shirt, preferably unbuttoned to show off what I imagined to be rock solid abs.

I was midway into my medication-induced sleep and fantasy about joining the mile high club with James, when I remembered a crucial bit of information from the brochure. There were three restaurants, two pools, and oh shit, an au naturel beach. Surely we wouldn't be going there!

24

Hot Hot Hot,
CARLOS SANTOS

"Wake up, Diana, wouldn't want you to miss the landing." I peered through the little window, spotted a postage stamp-sized island in the midst of turquoise waters, and wondered if there was enough room for a runway for the plane to land. I knew the stats: Grand Cayman was 76 square miles, had a population of about 50,000, and had well over 600 banks. With all those banks, where in hell was room for a runway?

"No worries, James," I mumbled as I crossed my fingers.

My ears popped as we dropped in altitude. The Lip Lady ignored us as she did a walk-through and checked for seatbelts. A couple of bumps later, we were on the ground. The planed braked hard. Engines whined, and the plane slowed to a stop. The crowd inside the plane applauded, myself included, even though I never understood why people did that. Hell, the pilot was getting paid for doing their job. Why was handclapping necessary? Then, that little girl from the seat in front dared to show her face. She looked pale and was gagging. I pulled the paper bag from James's seatback and held it in front of her mouth.

"Ha, gotcha," she said. "I was only pretending."

James laughed. The traitor!

Once on the ground, we joined the lineup for customs. I don't know why, but I always felt guilty, for some reason, going through a security check. It wasn't as if I was bringing any contraband onto the island, so perhaps it was just the sight of uniforms or watching too many television shows that dealt with border patrol.

"So, Diana, got anything to declare?" James asked.

"Nope. Do you?"

"I always travel light. Anything we need, we can pick up here."

Light? That sounded like police lingo. A gun maybe? Shit, why hadn't my course come with a detective dictionary? I was left wondering what he meant. Since we were near the officials, I reckoned mentioning the *gun* word would have both of us hauled off to an interrogation room. The officials signalled us forward, asked the required questions, stamped our passports, and waved us through. The sound of retching caught my attention, and I turned in time to see the little girl from the plane throwing up on the kid who'd slapped his mother. Had we been outside, I'd have acknowledged the sky and said, *Thanks, Mom.*

Brilliant sunshine welcomed us as we exited the terminal. The heat took my breath away, and James pointed at a compact black limousine. "That's ours," he said.

Huh, I was thinking. Already my mauve floral Wally Mart suitcase was being loaded into the trunk, and the rear door was held open by a very tall, very muscular, very handsome man. He gave James one of those man hugs, kind of like a back slap, and said, "Long time no see. Great to have you here, buddy."

"Likewise," said James. "Randy, this is Diana Darling. She's the other PI working the case with me, and she's a pro."

"Diana, it's my pleasure." Randy eyed me top to bottom, shook my hand, and kept holding it.

He was way too easy on the eyes. Shaved head and looked like he'd just stepped off the cover of GQ. Eyes that were way too intense. A black buttoned down shirt and tight black pants that outlined his assets. He had one of those military bearings that made me want to bow down or at least salute.

James coughed, gave Randy the eye, and said, "We'll debrief on the way to the hotel."

The air conditioning inside the limo helped clear my head. Randy was rattling off a report, "Isadora and Nigel cleared customs a few days back. They're using fake last names and the forged documents were good enough to get them through. I've booked you into a hotel next door to them. Your rooms will be overlooking the main entrance, so you can keep tabs on them coming and going. My secretary is sifting through some social media websites, and it looks like they've already created some profiles. I'll fill you in on that later. These are definitely kinky people. The banking information you were asking about earlier hasn't led anywhere yet. But I'm still working on it."

"Thanks, man. That's more than I was expecting." James turned to look at me. "Sorry, Diana, I should have explained earlier. Randy and I've worked a couple of cases before, plus we served together in the Middle East. I called him yesterday before the flight was booked."

"That's okay," I said. In my head, I was thinking he could have shared this crucial bit of information, but on the other hand, I hadn't always been totally transparent with him either. It was a fair trade. Randy was rattling off a few more details. My ears perked up when I heard the word *gun*.

"Will you require one or two?" Randy asked.

His voice was so casual, it almost sounded like he was asking, "Do you want fries with that?" Obviously I had a lot to learn about these guys and their history.

James turned to look at me, cocked an eyebrow, and replied. "Just one should do it. Diana's preferred weapon is pepper spray."

Randy's head veered to look at the rear-view mirror. Sunglasses hid his eyes, but there seemed to be a hint of a smile on his face. "One gun, one canister of pepper spray coming up, no problem."

The limo took an abrupt right turn, and we were headed down a narrow alley. God forbid another car would drive in the opposite direction because there sure as hell wouldn't be enough room for both of us. A few more turns, then Randy pulled the car to a stop, on a crumbled bit of sidewalk and in front of a rundown-looking shack. The overhead sign read, *Joe's Diner and More*.

It kind of reminded me of Shooters, except the guy inside was a lot taller than Rambo. There were no tables, so I presumed it was a takeout joint. Except for the fact there were no menus and not even a chalkboard indicating the feature item of the day. Guess that should have been my clue.

James leaned over the counter and ordered, "We'll have a Saturday night special and some compressed hot sauce on the side.

Cash exchanged, and then, ten minutes later we left. James had his gun, and my pepper spray came in a nice little compact purse decorated with palm trees. I hoped I didn't need to use it, but if push came to shove, this time I'd remember to aim away..

"So here's the set-up." Randy nodded at me, making sure I was included in the conversation. "Isadora and Nigel have rented a budget car. Presume they want to keep a low profile. I've already installed a tracking device, so we can keep tabs on them without getting too close."

"Perfect," said James. "You always were one step ahead. Probably what's kept you breathing over all these years."

Ooh, sounded like the boys had been in some nasty scrapes before, and I was dying to know what they were talking about, but decided this time I might learn more if I kept my mouth shut. Now if I could just manage it!

"The three of us will work a forced teaming sting," Randy continued. "We'll get their attention that way."

A forced teaming sting. What that hell was that? It sounded painful, and I wasn't sure this was what I'd signed up for. James must have caught me wince.

"Don't worry, Diana. All we're going to do is set up a scenario where Isadora and Nigel will need our help. Something like a minor fender bender or a situation where we appear to rescue them. It won't hurt to throw in something a little illegal, like a driving under the influence charge. Then we rescue and befriend them. Works all the time."

Wow, this was excellent! Way better than my course. A real-world job was where the training actually took place. I couldn't wait.

25

The Sting,
MARVIN HAMLISCH

James checked us into the hotel, and I carefully eyed the room. One large king-size bed, a small kitchenette area, and an ocean view from the balcony. It was perfect. I'd be comfortable enough, but I wasn't so sure about James. The couch didn't appear to be a pullout, and I was kind of hoping we'd be sharing a bed. But then he opened a door that led to an adjoining room. It was similar in layout, but had two twin beds instead, and the rest was a massive display of computers and other technical equipment. Randy entered through the main door, carrying a large duffel bag that clinked when he set it on the floor. "Got everything you asked for. Next time bring some lighter gear though, would ya?"

"Hey, you know me, man, nothing but the best," James said.

"Yeah, some things never change," Randy said as he eyed me. There was a grin on his face, and I wondered what I was missing here. I couldn't wait to have a side chat with Randy to pick his brain and learn more about James. Realistically, I knew very little about James, except that he runs a successful business, has a crazy ex-wife, and seems to have my cat eating out of his hand. There had to be more. A whole lot more.

"So when do we start, James?" I asked.

"Well, if you're up to it, we could plan the operation for later this afternoon. A lot will depend on the couple we're after. If they take a side trip, or go out in their car, that's our opportunity."

"What are we going to do, James? Run them over?"

"Nah, that's Randy's job."

My eyes must have been bulging out of my head because he quickly added, "Don't worry, Diana. Like I said, it's just going to be a minor fender bender. Randy knows how to play it. You and I get to rescue them. That's it. Once they feel beholden, they'll want to get to know us better. All we have to do is pretend we're a couple, be a bit naive, insinuate we have a few shady dealings of our own, and hope they take the bait."

My accounting brain was already creating a spreadsheet on the odds of our success. It seemed pretty good. "So what are we going to do if we catch them and get insight into their banking practices? It's not like we can arrest them."

"We can't, but Randy's got some people lined up here to handle that aspect of it. Let's be honest, they've faked their deaths by putting a couple of bodies in Isadora's car and burning it. God only knows they probably dug the bodies up from a cemetery somewhere or stole them from a mortuary where unidentified people are stacked. Reagan's already checking into that possibility. Next, they've bilked a bunch of people out of their life savings with that scam Nigel was running."

"So," I said, "all we need is a big confession, get the dirt on them, and turn them over to the police." Damn, that's when I realized I left my spy camera pen at home. Not good planning, but given the array of technology in the 2nd hotel room, it likely didn't matter.

"You're smart, Diana. That's exactly it. Once we get the dirt on them, our next biggest challenge will be getting them onto a boat and into international waters, close to the US coast, where we can have them arrested. Doesn't make sense to arrest them in the Cayman Islands when the crimes were committed back home. Deportation takes forever, and I'd like to see some of those victims get their money back, sooner rather than later."

I nodded. James has a good heart, plus he always seemed to be a couple steps ahead of me. It was perfect, and I was learning from a pro.

"Hey, they're heading out," Randy's voice interrupted. "Just got a call from the hotel's concierge, and they asked for directions to a bar farther up the coast. I've been there before, and it's kind of an underground banker-buddy bar. Sounds like they're making some connections for under-the-table deals."

James nodded. "I knew you were the man."

"You can follow them in my car. I've got a rust bucket we can use for the collision, after they've had a few drinks, and we'll take it from there," Randy said.

Yikes, it was all happening so quickly, and I was pretty sure I needed to change my clothes first. Wrinkled airline attire didn't suit undercover work.

"Want to do a quick change?" asked James.

Damn, this guy could read my mind. I nodded.

"You have anything low-cut in the front, just to show a bit of cleavage for Nigel?" He winked.

"Guess you'll have to wait and see," I said.

Two could play this game.

...

I carefully donned a pair of tight capri-style pants and a low-cut red silk top that easily showed two inches of cleavage—more if I bent over. I sprayed a light mist of perfume on my neck, applied lip gloss, swept my hair into an updo, and was ready to go.

Randy glanced up from his computer screen, a map with blinking targets on it, stifling a low wolf whistle—the kind I used to get when I was younger. It made me feel wanted, and that was a good feeling. James simply nodded, but out of the corner of my eye, I noticed a look between the two men. It was hard to decipher, but I think or maybe hoped it could be interpreted as *hands off.*

James grabbed the car keys. Randy left to trail behind Isadora and Nigel on their way to the bar and then set up for the return drive. He assured us there was a perfect stretch of road. Would be low speed because of a sharp turn, at an intersection, and it could happen there. We only needed to wait. There would be no major injuries. James and I would just have to swoop in. Now I was catching the drift of forced teaming sting. It was a new concept for me, but one that made a lot of sense.

Two hours later, I was getting restless. We were sitting in the car near a crossroad, by a bend in the road. James had his peaked cap pulled low over his eyes and was dozing off. How in hell could he be so relaxed? I, on the other hand, was keyed up to the max. So much for prying information out of him. Mind you, I'd probably have better luck getting blood out of a stone than getting details from him.

I'd already drunk my water bottle and half of James's. A mistake because now I really needed to pee. I crossed my legs, determined to hold it in. I'd read somewhere that your bladder can hold up to 17 or 18 ounces, a bit more than the size of a pint of beer, but you start to feel the urge to pee a lot earlier. *Could a bladder burst?* I wondered.

Damn, I crossed my legs again, determined to hold it in. James shifted in his seat, giving me a side look. "There aren't any bathrooms here, but there is a large tree about fifty feet away. Go for it." His cheek was doing that tweaking thing again. Darn, this guy was more psychic than my mother. She would have loved him!

...

I'd just returned from the outdoor bathroom facilities, when the cell phone rang. James put it on speaker, and Randy's voice crackled through. "Okay, we're good to go. They had more than a few cocktails, met with another couple in banker suits, and are just picking up the tab. Nigel's looking all happy and has a stupid, silly grin on his face. Man can't hold his liquor for sure. And Isadora just flashed the bartender. This should go down as planned. ETA is in twenty."

James drove the limo closer to the intersection and pulled to one side of the road. Minutes later, we saw the approaching vehicle, weaving along the lane. Randy's rust bucket lurched into action and nailed them broadside. Brakes screeched, followed by the unmistakable grinding of metal on metal. The smell of burning rubber drifted through my open window. Both vehicles came to a halt.

Randy leapt out, arms waving. Cripes, I'd never have even recognized him. Gone was the GQ man. Instead he looked like paunchy tourist wearing a shirt decorated with palm trees, baggy shorts, and a straw hat.

"Goddamn asshole," Randy shouted. "What the hell were ya doing? Didn't ya see the fuckin' stop sign?"

"What *shtop* sign?" Nigel threw his door open and staggered out. Even from where we were parked, his voice sounded slurred.

I'd never seen Nigel before and was less than impressed. An overweight man with squinty eyes, a bad orange comb-over that lifted in the breeze, and shorts that displayed fat knobby knees.

"Now what James?" I asked.

"Wait for Randy to do his thing. He'll give me the signal."

We watched as Isadora climbed out of the car. She was the exact opposite of Nigel. Impeccably dressed in a maroon blouse, an ankle-length matching skirt that flowed in the breeze, and holy shit, she was dripping with baubles. It looked like she'd pulled out everything from her jewellery box and put it on. Earrings, bracelets, necklaces, and rings on four out of five fingers, on each hand.

Randy and Nigel were toe to toe. Would have been eye to eye if Randy hadn't had a full six inches on him.

"The stop sign you just went through, you moron!" Randy was practically spitting in his face. He raised an arm to reposition his hat, and immediately James got out of the car. Ah, the signal.

James sauntered over to Nigel. "Hey what's going on here? You guys alright?" He also addressed Isadora who, by now, was leaning against the trunk of the car.

"Yes, I'm fine," Isadora said.

"Dammit, think I have whiplash." Randy rubbed the side of his neck. "Hope you guys have good insurance coverage."

Nigel's face took on a confused look, before turning all-knowing. "You're a scam artist. Ain't getting nothing from me."

"Ya, but you've been drinking. You reek of it. Who do ya think the cops are gonna believe?" Randy reached into his pocket and pulled out a phone, but hesitated. "The island cops hate tourists who drink and drive. Who do you think they're gonna believe?"

Nigel looked ready to back down, when James interrupted. "Saw the whole thing. Looks like you deliberately rammed him," James drawled as he turned to face Randy. James had pulled out his Texan accent again.

"And just who the hell are you?" Randy asked.

"Just a concerned bystander." James flashed a badge.

Randy winced, repositioned his hat, looked down, and shuffled his feet. "Sorry, sir, suppose it's possible I was mistaken." He mumbled, then skedaddled off to the rust bucket, put it in gear, and disappeared.

I got out of the limo and hurried over.

"You a cop?" Nigel was asking James.

"Far from it. Just a badge I bought online. It's helped me get out of a few scrapes before. You sure you guys are okay?"

Isadora kept silent. Nigel nodded and said, "Looks like I owe you huge. Thanks! How can I make it up to you?"

"No worries, I'm familiar with scam artists like that asshole. Your car still looks roadworthy. Not sure you should be driving though. Where y'all staying?" James asked.

"It's the Park Wood hotel and resort."

"What do ya know? That's right next to us. Tell ya what. I'll pull your car to the side of the road, let us drop you off, and you can pick it up from here later."

"Sounds like a plan," Isadora said, climbing into the back seat, and I followed alongside her. Nigel weaved his way into the passenger seat, looking relieved. I still had difficulty picturing Isadora and Harold as a couple, and Nigel and Bambi seemed an even further stretch. No amount of elastic in the world would have stretched enough to explain how these couples had got together.

The ride back was mostly silent. Nigel exhaled a lot of rum fumes, and it was making me heady. Every once in a while, Nigel would turn around, as if to make conversation. His mouth would gape, like a fish out of water, but very little substance would come out. The third time, Isadora caught him ogling my cleavage and swatted the back of his head. After that, his eyes remained glued to the road ahead.

We dropped them off with plans to meet the next day for lunch. I wondered if they would even remember. As they stumbled out of sight, James pumped a fist into the air, looked at me, and said, "That, Diana Darling, was a perfect forced teaming sting. Now, all we have to do is let it play out."

Inside the hotel room, Randy and James high-fived. "That was awesome. Looks like you haven't lost your touch."

"Trust me," said James, "the last thing those two feel will be my touch. And it will involve putting them behind bars, where they belong."

His tone gave me tingles. Wow, what a man.

"So what's next?" I asked.

"Well, we'll need to get our story straight, in case they start asking questions."

"Okay, things like how we met, how long we've been together. That kind of stuff?"

"Way ahead of you guys," Randy said.

He was busy divesting himself of the ugly palm tree shirt, and I spotted the rice bag taped to his torso that explained the earlier bulge. Damn, it looked heavy. He ripped it off, duct tape included. No evidence of pain, even though I'm sure it must have hurt. What was left was the epitome of a woman's dream date. Washboard abs, muscular biceps, and if it wasn't for the baggy shorts, he could have been on a poster for one of Arnold Schwarzenegger's bodybuilding contests. Arnie used to wear those little skimpy thongs for shows, so I wondered what was really underneath Randy's shorts. That's when I noticed. Randy's hands were huge!

26

Hey Bartender,
THE BLUES BROTHERS

By the next morning, I was fully drilled on the backstory for James and me. Plus, there'd been nothing else to do except read through the file folder, after James and Randy retired to the twin beds in the adjoining room.

According to the background information sheet, James and I had met at a swinging singles club in Las Vegas after a night of gambling. It had only been six months ago, which left us with a plausible reason, to explain to Isadora and Nigel, that we may not really know each other all that well. That made a lot of sense to me. Plus, apparently I was an heiress who had never worked, while James was a real estate developer with tons of money and huge property holdings in Florida. His specialty was the 55-plus age group, as he set up park homes and overcharged for land fees, insurance, and commodities. It was the perfect cover, and one that Nigel should easily identify with. Now, if we could just pull them in and get an admission of wrongdoing, we'd be fine.

There was a knock on the door from the adjoining room. "You up yet, Diana?"

"Sure, James, come on in." I was kind of disappointed Randy wasn't with him. James must have caught my glance over his shoulder. "Randy's in the process of following up with Reagan. It's not great news. Looks like a couple of bodies were excavated from a cemetery near the ravine where Isadora's car was found."

I caught the expression on his face, concerned, grim, yet still totally focused. I slumped down on the couch as this information was a blow to my gut. Wow, these people were evil. Even worse than I'd suspected. Who on earth would ever dig up bodies and burn them? My heart felt sick, my stomach roiled, tears welled up in my eyes, and I grabbed a tissue. This wasn't a game anymore. James sat down beside me and put an arm around my shoulder. "It's okay, we'll get them."

I had no answer, just silence. Still processing what I'd just heard.

"I've been there before. I understand what you're going through. Apprehending the bad guys can take a personal toll." He pulled me closer. No further comments. No questions. Just more silence. It was oddly comforting.

My head spun, replaying all the events that had led us here. The connections, the subterfuge, the interference with unknown people at a cemetery, and that's what pissed me off the most—those people deserved to be at peace. Up until now, I considered this role playing. Well, except for when James got nailed with the stun gun. That was serious stuff. Otherwise, it had been kind of fun. Now it was real life, and there was no going back for me.

Five minutes later, James finally spoke. "Tell you what. Nigel called about half an hour ago. He and Isadora want to meet us downstairs for lunch at the patio bar. If you need more time or want to back out, that's okay. I get it."

People's lives mattered, and I could make a difference. I, Diana Darling, could and would handle this. I gently removed his arm from my shoulder, looked him straight in the eye, and said, "No fucking way. These guys are going down!"

Then I stood up, brushed a tear from my eye, and inhaled. It was time to switch gears and get back into work mode. I contemplated what to wear for lunch with the pair of devils incarnate. Something red seemed appropriate.

"I'll be ready in fifteen minutes. Call the bastards back and accept," I said.

He nodded. "Love your stamina, Diana. Love your style."

I ruminated about his voice as I went through my clothes. Thank God Bambi's sister had steered us to the brightly coloured section in the middle of the Clothes Barn. I had the perfect outfit: a fire-engine red halter top and a matching full-length skirt with a slit exposing the upper thigh. It was time for justice.

...

James and I met in the stairwell before heading down to the bar. His eyes were kind, thoughtful, but I couldn't ignore the appraising look he gave me.

"Just remember," James said, "stick to the script from Randy in case they start asking questions that are more personal. Otherwise, we'll let things fall into place."

The restaurant was outdoors and oceanside, with a bar in the middle, a thatched roof, some wicker-laced bar stools, and a dozen tables for diners. With a pool to the left and a jetty that stretched into the water, the setting would have been idyllic in any other circumstance. Patrons sunbathed in lounge chairs around the pool, others swam in the sea, and a small group was enjoying beverages at the far end of the jetty. Another perusal of the area confirmed Isadora and Nigel hadn't arrived yet. Good. Maybe she was still trying to extricate herself from the Velcro handcuffs she'd mentioned in the e-mails to Nigel. Damn, she belonged in real handcuffs, hard metal tight around her wrists and cuffed in the back.

James pulled out a bar stool for me, and I took a look at the drinks listed on the blackboard. Everything from piña coladas to cold brews, margaritas, and more, including a drink called the Teddy Dive—the special of the day. Alcohol would be a welcomed buffer against the tide of emotions that had just been unleashed upon me. The bartender's back was to us. Something seemed familiar about the way he moved, the way he grabbed the bottles and poured. Dancing and moving his hips in rhythm to the sound of calypso music blaring from the bar's speakers. That's when he turned around. Holy shit, I was right!

I carefully rescued my jaw before it hit the bar counter. "Teddy, what are you doing here?"

He moved in, his eyes dancing. "I could ask you the same thing, but since you're here, I get to thank you in person."

His tone still held that melodic hint, and the gleam in his eyes was hard to look away from. He reached across the bar and held my hand in both of his. I struggled to stay upright on my bar stool. "Thank me for what?" I asked.

"Just got a call from Bambi, and it looks like the kid ain't mine. Said she collected some DNA from a snot rag at some playground and sent it off to a lab. The lab compared it to mine, and the results came back today. Teddy, you are NOT the father," he said.

Fast turnaround, I thought. Wonder how much that would cost me!

"Oh that. No problem." I made a mental note to hit the bathroom, call Bambi, and thank her for being so resourceful. "So why are you here?" Teddy's sunglasses were still halfway down his nose, but he peered at me over the top. "Wait, let me guess. You're undercover again."

"Maybe. What about you?" I asked.

"Since the Muff Dive burned down, I've been out of work. My brother has a few tourist boats in the Cayman Islands, and I've been picking up extra cash as a captain. Tips at the bar help. Now, for you, and only you, there will be no tab." He winked. "The other guy," he said, nodding at James, "will be paying a premium. As I recall, he wasn't exactly a big tipper the last time I met him."

Teddy was still holding my hand, promising a sunset cruise for just the two of us. Reluctantly, I removed his hands from mine and whispered, "Yeah, we're undercover. Don't blow it for us."

He winked. "Anything for you, my darling, Diana."

I was in the midst of fantasizing about Teddy, a woman's dream for lipstick removal, when James nudged my knee. "They just arrived," he said, motioning over his shoulder to a set of stairs that led from poolside to the bar.

I glanced briefly, spotted Isadora and Nigel, ignored them, raised my voice, and said, "Well, bartender. What do you suggest?"

"The best drink on the island is the Teddy Dive special. It's a blend of rum and other ingredients that will remain secret. If you're looking for fruit and some of those tiny paper umbrellas', that can also be arranged." He glanced up. "Ah, looks like you're meeting friends. Shall I wait until you all decide?"

I swivelled around on the bar stool, spotted Isadora and Nigel approaching, and waved at them.

"Hey, guys! Glad you're here. The bartender is promising us a special drink. Care to partake?" I asked. Nigel nodded in assent, probably needing some *hair of the dog* after yesterday's overindulgence to keep him from going through withdrawal symptoms.

Isadora's perfume wafted towards me. Christ, had she taken a bath in the stuff? She was still three feet away, and I could already smell her. It was like a Chanel No. 5 knockoff, or it could have been the Evening in Paris one that came in a little purple bottle with a tassel. Nigel was holding her hand, a few steps behind. Probably still in the doghouse after ogling my cleavage yesterday. I gave the girls a shake, made sure they were well-positioned in my V-neck halter, and was ready for action.

James rose, greeted them both, and assisted Isadora to a bar stool beside mine, while he and Nigel stood behind us. Nigel grasped his hand and went into a litany of thanks for yesterday's rescue until James interrupted.

"Stop right there. Not necessary. We're here to enjoy the day," James said.

I chose that moment to cross my legs, making sure the slit in my skirt was as high up as it could possibly go. The men's eyes travelled, and meanwhile I engaged Isadora in a conversation. Starting with, "You okay from yesterday?" I then launched into the usual: where are you from, how long are you staying, have you been here before, etc. All the required bullshit designed to make her feel comfortable with me.

As she started to respond, Teddy arrived with four massive drinks in towering glasses that could easily have held my bladder contents from yesterday, in other words about 18 ounces. Ice cubes bobbled and bounced as we all clinked glasses. *Mmm, liquid lunch*, I wondered. But then again, James always seemed to know when I was hungry. No worries on that front. Teddy passed us some brochures promising a three-hour boat tour, courtesy of his brother.

Twenty minutes into our superficial dialogue, it happened. James's phone rang. He slightly turned away, mumbled something about bank account numbers, and berated the caller for not having already known about when to sell the damn stocks. Then, more about a deposit and making sure it was covered. Nigel's ears immediately went on high alert. He reminded me of Xena when she heard the crinkle of the cat treat bag being opened. Things were unfolding according to plan.

27

Suspicious Minds,
ELVIS PRESLEY

Thanks to the flow of liquor and Teddy's expertise at customer service, Isadora was starting to preen herself for Teddy. She licked her lips. A slow tongue circling the rims. Then, she proceeded to run her fingers through her hair and toss her head to the side while she gazed at him with utter fascination. As I watched, the whole image of her being a classy lady spiralled down the drain. Even a plumber with one of those electric drain snakes wouldn't be able to retrieve the earlier image I had of her. Nigel gave her a nudge, pointing at a couple items on the food menu. "Okay, sounds good," Isadora gushed.

Nigel seemed to be at a different pace, hurriedly indicating a nearby dining table. The message was clear. It was time to eat.

We were partway through a Cayman-style conch stew with rice, a side salad, and the coconut shrimp Isadora had insisted upon after being seated, when James's phone rang again.

"Dammit! Sorry, guys. I really need to take this."

I watched Nigel's eyes follow James; his ears straining as if to pick up on the conversation. This call took longer, and Isadora and I finished our meal by the time he returned.

"Problems?" Nigel asked.

"Yes and no. I'm just not familiar with the banking stuff down here. Man, it's complicated."

"It can be if you don't know the right people." Nigel was starting to look totally intrigued. "If you want, I might be able to help you out. I've got some experience here myself in the industry. Could maybe introduce you to the right people."

"Well, I'm not sure," James hesitated. "Some of my dealings are not exactly . . ." His voice trailed off as he waved the back of his hand in the air.

"It's okay. Think I might understand where you're at. Besides, I owe you one from yesterday."

Still, James waited. I knew he was playing it to the hilt, plus I knew the phone calls were from Randy, and the response required perfect timing. God only knows what they were really talking about—probably Randy's view of the pool and the bikini-clad women.

Nigel's eyes shifted back to his plate, as if he were done with the conversation. That's when James chimed, "That could be a really good idea. Perhaps you can offer some advice."

Nigel beamed. "Ladies, why don't you go back to the bar while James and I discuss business?"

"No problem. You coming, Diana?" Isadora was already getting up, tossing her napkin on the table.

"Sure, just gotta hit the ladies' room first," I said.

Isadora made a beeline to the bar, perched on a bar stool right in front of Teddy, and was continuing her earlier lip licking and eye rolling. God, she was like a cat in the heat! The only thing missing was the persistent *yowls*.

In the bathroom, I pulled out my phone from my little palm tree purse that also contained the pepper spray, and I called Bambi. She answered on the first ring. "So have you laid him yet?"

Huh? I was wondering. "Laid who?"

"Geez, Diana, sometimes I really wonder about you. I'm talking about James."

"We're on a case, and it's business."

"Yeah right, like I'm really going to believe that? Anyways, just in case you're wondering, Xena is fine. Seems to like the Whispering Pines motel and has Harold down to a fine art. He's in her clutches. He even went shopping for new cat toys and a long feather on a stick to play with her. It tickles," Bambi giggled.

Cripes, I wanted to erase the whole scenario from my mind and hoped Xena was under the bed, not a willing witness to their folly.

"So back to business," I said. "Teddy's working here at our hotel bar. Tells me you've cleared up the paternity case. Just how much did the expedited DNA testing cost?" I asked.

"Don't worry, pulled in a favour from a friend. We got the discounted rate, and it'll go on his tab. Besides, Teddy's brother is loaded, owns a bunch of tourist boats, and even an ocean liner. You should ask for an introduction."

Good Lord, I was thinking. How many friends did this woman have? She was bringing in customers, provided free clothes, knew people who analyzed DNA, and was a cat sitter. Damn, I was smart to hire her.

As I headed back to the bar, James and Nigel seemed to be in deep discussion at the dining table. Isadora, on the other hand, was still flirting with Teddy. I caught his glance. It registered something along the lines of *please save me from this woman*.

Since we might need to make use of his brother's boat, I hurried to the bar to give Teddy a reprieve. As Teddy smiled at me, Isadora frowned and ordered another drink. Obviously this woman didn't handle competition well.

"Ya know what, Diana. There's something familiar about your voice. Feel like I've talked with you before."

"I hear that all the time. Must be the mid-coast accent," I lied.

"No, it's more than that." She paused, peering at me with discerning eyes, albeit somewhat rum-glazed. "Just can't quite put my finger on it."

Yikes, had my cover just been blown? James and I'd agreed to keep first names. Our names weren't exactly out of the ordinary. Given we'd never met either of our clients in the flesh, it had seemed like the best plan.

"Well, I'm sure if I met you before, I'd remember it. You're a classy lady and pretty hard to miss," I said. Then, I waited. Her earlier suspicions seemed to lessen. Looks like flattery could get you almost everywhere. She meandered in conversation, and I sat back and let her drive the chat. Teddy was seeking refuge at the opposite end of the bar, but I noticed he kept glancing in our direction.

It seemed like time for some private investigator stuff, so I started asking Isadora about Nigel.

"So it sounds like your guy understands the banking industry here?"

Her left eyebrow rose, making her look like a really bad caricature of a press secretary I'd seen on the news recently. Yikes, I needed to back off.

"Nigel's a smart guy. That's why we're together. I don't get why you're asking about that?" Her earlier suspicious look had just returned.

I raised my left arm, as if to stretch, and made sure James noticed. It was our signal that I needed help. His approach provided a further distraction as he came towards the bar.

"That's one good-looking guy you're hooked up with there," Isadora said, switching her focus to James in a nanosecond. She eyed him the way someone would the first time they see a Corvette—instant love or lust.

For a short time, I almost felt sorry for Nigel, but his expression seemed to indicate he couldn't have cared less. Or maybe he was just used to it.

"So I'm going to steal James for a few hours tomorrow. Have him meet some business friends of mine. Maybe you two ladies could find something special to do," Nigel said.

Isadora still kept her eyes on James, mentioned something about a nude beach or a spa day or some other entertainment that combined all three.

I tried not to look alarmed. Visiting a nude beach with this lady was not on my To-Do List. The spa I could handle, and God only knew what she meant by *other entertainment*. Then, she winked at me and nodded towards Teddy. Good Lord, was she thinking about a threesome?

James spoke up, "I'm sure y'all will find something good to occupy your time. Should only be a few hours. I'm meeting Nigel around noon."

As we left the bar, Isadora waved. Teddy's brother's boat pamphlet was clutched in her hand. "I'll call you in the morning, so we can make plans. What's your last name, Diana?"

My automatic response was to say Darling. My mouth opened, but I managed to constrain myself and held back. Cripes, that would have totally blown our cover all to hell. James took control.

"No problem. Nigel has our room number from yesterday. You can just call that."

I gripped his hand, waiting until we were out of earshot before I said, "Damn, that was close. Force of habit I guess."

"Happens to all of us," he said. "Great that you were able to keep silent."

For once in my life, I'd been able to keep my mouth shut.

...

We reconvened back in Randy's room. James went immediately to the computer screens. "So what do we have here?"

"Well, I've wired Nigel and Isadora's room for sound. Any conversation they have will be recorded. Maybe we'll get a hit on some of his banking connections. Plus, I just got off the phone with Reagan about Andrew and seems like he's a bit of a turncoat," Randy said.

"How so?" James was hovering over my shoulder, but he addressed Randy.

"It looks like he's turned tail. Even confessed about his connection and the shady business dealings with his so-called high school buddies. He's already been in front of a judge. Will be kept in jail until his sentencing. No unauthorized contact with Nigel or Isadora unless it's taped and recorded. Andrew's in agreement for a lighter sentence." Then, Randy turned to me and said, "Also, found a brochure for you, Diana, just in case you need it."

Huh? I was thinking. What did he mean? He passed a printout to me, titled "Good Nude Beach Etiquette."

"It's always good to be prepared," he said with a wink.

How in hell did he know about Isadora's proposed visit to an au naturel beach? Then, I remembered these guys were pros. I was just a novice. Damn, I had so much to learn. I glanced at James as if to say, *I'm not doing this*. But he and Randy were deep in conversation—one of those buddy-guy things. It royally pissed me off. Actually, it made me wish I had a female counterpart to compare notes with. I was really missing Bambi out here, and she was too far away for a face-to-face.

James muttered something about a meeting in the morning to plan the next day. Randy went on about more surveillance. I'd had enough.

Screw the guys. I headed back to my room. Reckoned there would be no new wardrobe coming my way. After all, a nude beach didn't exactly require clothes.

28

Stormy Weather,
LENA HORNE

I ordered room service for dinner, sprawled out on the couch, and picked up the dreaded brochure. It was titled, "Important things to know regarding nude beach etiquette," and it reminded me of David Letterman's Top Ten List segment on his TV show. This Top Ten List should be titled, "All things that should be totally avoided if at all possible."

Number 1: Ensure the beach you are at is definitely a nude beach. *Like duh, how could someone miss something so obvious?*

Number 2: If you're not sure and you're going with friends, do not be the first person to take off all your clothes. They may run away with them. These people are definitely not friends.

Number 3: Don't forget about sunburn. Remember that certain parts of your body may have never before been exposed to these kinds of rays. Apply sunscreen before going out. You don't want to be rubbing yourself in public.

Number 4: Keep your eyes to yourself. Remember, everyone has seen it all before. If you can't comply, wear a really good pair of mirrored sunglasses to hide behind.

Number 5: Trim down and keep it tidy. *Since I'd already had to trim down at the couples retreat when I borrowed James's razor, I reckoned this was a no-brainer.*

Number 6: Remember, there are insects in the air and creatures in the sand and the water. *Crap, if I had to go through with this, I was planning on hiding out in the water. Damn, did the Cayman Islands have jellyfish? I knew they had stingrays, and the last scenario I needed were those slimy legs wrapped around my private parts. This just kept getting worse!*

Number 7: Bring something to do. A book to read, cards to play with, or something to keep you occupied. You don't want your hands to wander. *Now realistically, this sounded really obscure. You're going to a nude beach and bringing cards. It's not like you're going to play strip poker here. Duh!*

Number 8: Guys, never go with someone you're attracted to. No further explanation required on that one.

Number 9: Leave your camera at home. *Mmn. I spent the next 15 minutes thinking about hiding my spy camera pen in my ponytail and positioning it upright to view the scenery. Then, I remembered I'd left it at home. Total waste of time.*

Number 10: Remember it's a nude beach. Enjoy the freedom and the air. Other participants are not there to watch you and your partner. Get to know each other better. If you feel the need for private shenanigans, then you should just get a room.

...

That night I fell into a fitful sleep. Tossed, turned, and dreamt of naked people on a beach. Some were people I recognized, like Dave, the owner of the Muff Dive. Next, was Tribal Tits, aka Deborah attired only in nipple tassels, and finally the security guard, who truly did have hair sprouting from everywhere. Others were faceless beings, and I practiced looking down, only saw feet. It was a nightmare!

I awoke to find the bed totally stripped. Sheets, a blanket, and pillows were all in a tangled mess on the floor. There was a term I recalled learning from an English teacher when I was in a grade ten writing class. The term was *foreshadowing*, a.k.a. portending things to come. I glanced at the now naked bed. *Please don't let this happen now*, I begged. Through the partially open blinds, it still looked somewhat dark outside, but I leapt off the mattress, grabbed the sheets from the floor, and quickly remade the bed. My attempt to interrupt the foreshadowing and foil whatever the day would bring. It was worth a try!

There was a knock on the door from the adjoining room, then James said, "You decent, Diana?"

I glanced down before responding. Yup, kitty pyjamas covered me. Before Bambi and I went to the Clothes Barn, I hadn't even considered the whole lingerie thing. Mind you, wearing other peoples underwear didn't seem like a good fit. Perhaps it was worth a return trip to the Clothes Barn when I got home, though I'd only purchase the lingerie that still had price tags on them.

"Sure, James. Come on in."

"Looks like you got a reprieve."

Huh? I was wondering.

"Have you looked out the window?" James asked.

Randy followed James into the room and drew the blinds fully open, just as a crack of thunder reverberated through the air. Relief flooded through me. Waves crashed on the shoreline. Palm trees bent and twisted under the wind. Rain poured down in torrents. As my mother would say, "A storm is a well-choreographed dance of Mother Nature." It also meant the whole nude beach thing was now out of the question.

"Thank you, Mom," I whispered as I moved onto the balcony, leaning over the railing and welcoming the downpour that whisked leeside by the winds.

"Uh, aren't you getting wet out there?" Randy seemed to be eyeing my wet kitty pyjama top. "Hey, it's no different than standing in the shower. Only difference is the temperature of the water. Speaking of which, when I do get out of the real shower, there should be breakfast. Preferably crispy bacon and poached eggs, with Hollandaise sauce on some well-toasted English muffins."

James nodded at Randy. "This girl marches on her stomach. Let's get it done."

Randy tore his eyes away from my chest and headed to the kitchenette. James's eyes lingered. I headed to the shower. The one with warm running water. But I reckoned in this case, cold water might be required.

...

Partway through breakfast, the phone rang. James motioned for me to pick it up, with the speaker on.

"Hello," I said.

"Isadora here. Looks like the weather's not cooperating today for a nude beach get-together."

"Too bad," I sighed, trying to sound disappointed. Relief was welcomed instead. Hell, I probably would have chosen poking hot needles into my eyes versus doing the beach thing with her. "What about the spa thing you mentioned?"

"Well, apparently my favourite massage guy is off today. So I've come up with something completely different," Isadora said.

Randy and James nodded at me to reply. "So tell me, what's up?"

"I've found a lady here who is touted as being the best psychic and card reader on the island. I've already booked us two appointments, and a driver will pick us up at noon."

James was already motioning me to say *no*. Randy was waving his hands in the air, as if to say, *what the hell, don't go there*.

I ignored them both. "Sounds great," I said. "What's her name?"

"It's Portia, and like I said, she is highly recommended."

I momentarily held the phone away from my mouth, breathed a sigh of relief before bringing it back, and responded, "Perfect, I'll be downstairs at noon. Looking forward to it." And I hung up.

James was still shaking his head. Randy gave me a look that read, *have you just gone off your rocker?*

"What if she's really psychic?" James asked. "It's not that I believe in that stuff, but we sure don't need our cover blown by some witch."

"It's okay, I can handle this. Trust me," I said. Besides, Portia was my grandmother's name. Looks like the women of my family were definitely looking out for me today.

29

Bette Davis Eyes,
KIM CARNES

The earlier downpour had now succumbed to a light shower. Skies still overcast, yet the wind was brisk. The driver dropped us off in front of something that closely resembled a circus tent—an orange and white striped pinnacle top, with canvas sides that, at best, had enough room to fit about ten customers. The driver promised to pick us up in a couple of hours and fled at a higher than normal speed. Led me to believe he was afraid of this Portia woman, and perhaps her reputation was as good as Isadora had claimed. The folded sidewalk placard read, "Tarot card readings, crystal ball gazing, palm reading, and more. Satisfaction guaranteed."

I wasn't afraid. Knew from my mom that most card readers fed off the reactions of the clients. Things like facial expressions, body language, verbal responses, and more. The big questions most customers asked had to do with love, money, health, and travel.

This whole set-up looked like trailer park witchery to me. Not a bona fide psychic. Besides, with no investment in a real building, she could pick up, pack up, and move on a whim, plus with very little overhead in terms of financing, if she accepted cash only, it was like free money in the bank. This was destined to be a walk in the park and a grateful reprieve from the hellish nude beach nightmare I'd endured last night.

"You coming Diana, or are you just going to stand outside and get wet?" Isadora asked.

"Yup, I'll be right on your heels." I moved under the awning, Isadora shoved the entry canvas curtain aside, and we entered.

Wow, this was not what I'd been expecting. I recognized the scent of Patchouli oil, while smoke wafted from incense stick burners resting on a stand. Items for sale included sage sticks for air cleansing, miniature glass crystal balls on key rings, and a myriad of other paraphernalia. The last time I'd attempted crystal ball gazing with Mom had resulted in me falling off a stool after staring too long and seeing nothing but smoke and mirrors. I think that's when she gave up on any witchcraft genes being passed on to me.

This place, however, looked more like a real store than the Clothes Barn. *Hmm*, I wondered. Maybe Witchcraft 101 wouldn't have been such a bad idea after all. This lady probably made a killing selling this stuff. I was so busy looking around that I almost tripped over a waist-high bong pipe that leaned against one of the counters. At the very least, I now knew what fuelled her so-called inner channelling. The hookah pipes on the counter were confirmation.

A long robed middle-aged woman with a flowered headscarf greeted us. "I'm Portia. Here to answer all your questions." She gave me a fleeting glance, seemed to dismiss me, then pointed at Isadora. "You 'vil be first for za reading. Follow me."

Isadora seemed to miss the lack of consistency in Portia's accent. I, on the other hand, immediately registered it as *phony*. As Portia led my all-too-eager companion to the rear, I noticed grass-stained bare feet under her long, flowing robe. Maybe it was an attempt at grounding after too much bong-pipe inhaling.

With Isadora safely ensconced in a rear section of the tent, I checked out the candle shelf. Every colour and shape imaginable, including one that resembled that personal elephant object I'd hidden in the ceiling tile at my office. Another display case featured potions that boasted labels, such as "How to make a man love you," "How to win the lottery," and even one that promised "Immediate weight loss." Yup, this woman was a fake.

Conversation spilled through the thin cloth curtain, and I realized that when it was my turn, I had to be careful. Everything could be heard. I moved closer, heard a bunch of mumbo jumbo, then a comment about *being careful about new friends you hook up with*, plus some stuff about her significant other and being able to trust him. Isadora asked about travel. Portia responded with, "I see an ocean venture in your near future. Be careful, it may not go as planned." More words I struggled to hear. Damn, now Isadora would be really suspicious of James and me. Perhaps this hadn't been such a good idea after all.

Thirty minutes later, the voices were more audible. It sounded like things were wrapping up, so I headed to the front of the tent. Didn't want it to look like I was eavesdropping. The damn bong pipe was staring me in the face. Had it been lit and fuelled, I may have taken a puff myself, just for courage.

When she finally returned from her reading, Isadora looked somewhat confused. I wasn't sure if that was a good sign or a bad one. "So how did it go?" I asked.

"Not what I was expecting. I need to think on things. Your turn next."

As I entered the area at the rear of the tent, Portia motioned me towards a round table draped with sheer black cloth. Tarot cards sat in the middle, alongside a clear crystal ball that had to be the size of a saucer. Candles were lit in all four corners of the area. It wasn't far off from the dining room set-up my mom had, while I was growing up, when she did readings for her clients, so setting-wise, it was kind of comfortable. I sat down on a chair across from Portia.

"Do you have any questions you need answered, or would you prefer a general reading?" Portia asked.

"General reading would be fine." No fake accent this time, I noticed.

Portia gave me a look. Piercing green eyes surrounded by smoky black eyeshadow penetrated my core. My gut lurched. An attempt at avoiding direct eye contact by focusing on the middle of her forehead wasn't working. It reminded me of the time I'd lied to Mom about spending the night with a girlfriend, when in reality it was the girlfriend's brother. Another damn mistake that had been 'cause Mom was never easily fooled, and I ended up spending the next two weeks on chore duty.

"One general reading coming up, but you already know how to do that, don't you? You really should have listened to your mother. Trusted in your own inherited abilities. She's watching over you," Portia said.

Crap, this Portia lady was the real deal! Now what? I looked for an escape. Best exit would be crawling under the canvas between a pair of tent pegs, but I wouldn't be able to fit through. Plus, that would leave Isadora behind. No fight or flight. I had to stay.

"It's okay. I'm not going to blow your cover. Not sure what you're really up to, but in the meantime, we'll spend some time here, and then you'll be buying some items from the gift store on the way out."

I nodded in assent, noticing that she kept her voice low so as not to be overheard.

"Lots and lots of merchandise," she whispered.

Thank God, James had given me his credit card before leaving the hotel. It seemed as if destiny was about to put one hell of a dent in our plans!

30

Night Moves,
BOB SEGER

It was mid-afternoon when the driver dropped me off at the hotel. Isadora had been mostly quiet on the way home, but her earlier suspicious look had been resurrected. I stumbled through the door carrying four overflowing bags of stuff I'd bought at the circus tent. After purchasing the third trinket, I'd tried to say *enough*. Portia wasn't having it until another bag was filled. Maybe I could hide them under the bed, so James wouldn't notice until he got his credit card bill. That's when I saw the sticky note on the door to my room. "Do Not Enter," it said. "Go to Randy's room."

It only took half a knock for the door to open. James had a headset positioned over his ears, with the cord dangling. Randy was sitting at one of the computers. "Looks like you went shopping instead of to a psychic," James said, smiling. "I take it you saw the note."

"I did. So what's up?" I asked.

"Looks like Nigel's a bit of a bugger."

"What do you mean?" I was starting to feel confused. What was I missing here?

"Well, he's arranged to have your room bugged with two cameras and audio. Randy picked up on it. Seems like Nigel wants to make sure we're legitimate before moving forward with business dealings. Or maybe he's a bit of a voyeur. Not quite sure."

"So, James, I take it your meeting went well with him?" *Please, oh please, don't ask me about my day with Isadora*, I was thinking. *Keep him sidetracked.*

No such luck.

"How did your day go?" James glanced at the bags. "Expensive?"

I shrugged. "Different than expected. Picked up some souvenirs."

Randy stood up from the desk, signalling James to plug in his headset, and handed me a pair. Once connected, I could hear the conversation between Isadora and Nigel.

She'd just gotten into her room and was chastising Nigel for making her spend time with *that stupid woman*, then went into a litany of stuff the psychic had told her. Bottom line, Nigel was fine with his meeting with James. But Isadora wasn't sure we were actually a couple. Made some comments about me being sexually incompetent and how I probably didn't even know how to really please a man. Where the hell she'd gotten that from, I had no idea. I presumed she didn't want Nigel near me, and that was just fine.

"So where do we go from here?" I asked, taking off the headset.

"There's a lot riding on this. We need to prove them wrong."

Holy crap, I thought. Randy grinned. James smiled. I, on the other hand, wished for a nude beach. Alone!

...

"You sure you're up for this, Diana?" James's tone was professional, but his cheek was doing that tweaking thing again. I'd come to recognize it, yet still could never figure out how to read him.

"You can back out anytime," James said.

"I can handle it. It's only acting, right?"

We already knew the room was bugged, so to maintain the profile Isadora and Nigel expected, James and I would have to prove we were really a couple. At lunch yesterday, Isadora had seemed suspicious. Today's visit with the psychic hadn't helped, and Nigel seemed to trust her judgment. Based on Randy's bug detector, we knew they set up surveillance in our room. There were two cameras—one on the combination ceiling fan and light over the bed, the second by the bedside clock radio. Plus, there were four listening devices throughout the room, including one on the balcony. Once the two cameras were disabled, it would come down to sound effects. I faked a lot of orgasms in my life, so how hard could it be this time?

We were outside the door to our hotel room. James held the keycard in his hand. Gave me one final look and swiped the plastic. I slipped off the straps of my tank top, ruffled my hair, and pinched my cheeks to elicit a red flush. Yup, I could play this out. The camera light turned green. No turning back. It was show time.

James opened the door and pulled me through. I jumped into his arms, wrapped my legs around his waist, and let him carry me. His hands held my hips in clutch mode. Heat seared through me. Had it not been for the cameras, I swear he might have been turned on, even just a little. His eyes danced, a smile crossed his lips, and he gave me a wink just before tossing me on the bed.

I squealed in delight. "Again, so soon. Are you sure?"

"Yah, maybe it's that couple. Gotta admit, they're a bit older, but damn, they seem like a team. Really well-connected. Maybe we could be like them one day, and I couldn't help but notice, Nigel struggled to keep his eyes off of you. Any idea how hot that makes me?"

This time I didn't need to manufacture the flush. It came readily. "Trust me, Isadora had her eyes on you, and it wasn't just your face she was looking at."

"Ah, a voyeur," he murmured. "A woman after my own heart."

"James, you've never told me you were into stuff like that."

"Guess we all have our fantasies, but for now you're here. And you're mine."

I was flat on my back, lying on the bed. James straddled my hips. I caressed his shoulder, nuzzled his neck with a few kisses, then slowly unbuttoned his God-awful flowered shirt and tossed it in the air, aiming at the ceiling fan. The shirt landed on the blades. Perfect, camera one was out of commission. I arched my back, stroked my sides, wiggled my hips, and gave James my best *come hither* look.

His eyes widened. I wasn't sure if it was my acting job, or if he was really getting turned on, but his shorts seemed to be at half-mast. I struggled to remind myself this was work, and there was still one more camera to go.

"So what do ya think, my sexy one. Do you want it slow and easy . . . or hard and fast?" I asked. James's eyes grew even wider. He grabbed the back of my neck, pulling me into a lip lock that seemed to last forever.

"This time, you're the boss." His voice sounded growly, sexy, and he threw in some heavy breathing. "I'll leave it up to you." His hand trailed under my tank top, stopping to rest between my breasts. Fingers tugged at my bra. "But that's gotta go."

Shit, his cheek was doing that tweaking thing it always does when he's toying with me. I mean, he's already seen me in a bikini top, and my bra provided more coverage. What the hell. So I slid my arms down, extricated myself from the tank top, and tossed it over the bedside alarm clock. Camera number two was now disabled. His breathing was still hard; I was feeling confused. But it was a job. And I could take one for the team. After all, he was the one paying the bill.

Now all we needed to do was fabricate the bump and grind sounds of love making and intercourse. He winked at me as he stood at the side of the bed and made a motion signifying a rolling film camera. It was my turn to talk.

"Damn, James, you're gonna have to get rid of those shorts. Please, let me help you," I murmured, then sighed and flicked the bed sheets through my hands to mimic the sound of clothes being removed. "Ah, you're perfect now. Just the way Mother Nature intended." I chose to ignore the fact that his shorts seemed to be saluting me. It was awkward for sure, but still I felt a hint of, Oh My God, this guy might really be turned on. The mind game was powerful stuff. Made me wonder how people did it in the movies, just for show.

We moved to opposite sides of the bed, sat, jumped up and down, and were rewarded with spring noises from the mattress. The sound effects were perfect.

"Ohh, James," I moaned. "I'm so ready for you now."

"Not so fast." A manufactured groan escaped from his lips. "We have lots of time."

"Are you sure? You don't look like a man who wants to wait. Besides, didn't you say I could be the boss this time?" I groaned low in my throat. "Now. I want you now."

James moved to the end of the bed, planted his foot on the mattress, and rhythmically thrust it until the headboard clattered against the wall. *That should do it*, he mouthed. "Sweetie, in my books you're always the boss. And now, it will be now."

I left James to continue thrusting. Mostly I just wanted to calm myself and ramp down the hormone level that encompassed me. I searched for the remote control, planning to turn on the TV's music station later. Maybe music would drown out some of the audio in the room. I knew there were four listening devices. One by the radio, one on the balcony, another in the bar area, and the last tied to the TV.

James was picking up the pace on the headboard banging and he pointed at me. "Now, please now. Come now," he shouted.

"Yes, God yes, oh James . . ." I screamed. I always thought simultaneous orgasms were overrated and only happened in movies. If so, we had just satisfied Nigel and Isadora. I was pretty sure they'd be impressed.

James removed his foot from the end of the bed. Fortunately, the headboard and wall were still intact. "Hope we didn't wake the neighbours," I giggled.

The audio was still on, so we had to keep up the pretense.

I pressed the power button on the TV remote, thinking that background noise might mask further conversation. Nothing happened. James was looking out the window at the ocean. I wasn't sure what he was thinking, but maybe he was doing a little unwinding of his own. I headed to the kitchenette. Apparently pseudo sex made me hungry. I was busy sorting through some crackers and cheese when he tackled me from behind. He hauled me into the bed and threw the covers over us. What the hell? Maybe he really did want me. I blossomed at the thought.

He pointed at the ceiling fan that was now starting a slow rotation. His shirt hung precariously to one of the blades. Shit, I must have hit a button for the damned fan. Camera one was about to come back into play.

"Now what?" I whispered.

His grin royally pissed me off. His lips were near my ear. "We can stay fully clothed under the covers until it gets dark. Or one of us can get naked and stroll around the room to turn off the lights." The fan had picked up speed, and James's shirt was blown to a nearby chair.

I glanced at the clock. It would be a full thirty minutes until sunset and darkness. Damn, no way was I getting undressed under the sheets and parading around for anyone else's prying eyes. "Ain't gonna be me," I whispered back.

"So, sweetie," he murmured, just loud enough for the listening device. The back of James's head was facing the camera on the ceiling fan. "Any chance you can catch a second wind before we meet Isadora and Nigel for drinks. I promised Nigel we'd meet him at the bar tonight."

My face was a full frontal towards camera one. Two could play this game. I rolled him on his back before saying. "Save it for later, lover." I couldn't tell if he was happy or disappointed. For the next while, we rested, sort of . . . and waited until darkness fell.

An hour later, I changed into one of those free flowing island dresses. Loose around the hips, but low-cut and tight around the bosom. I sprayed a mist of perfume, walked through it so the scent wouldn't be too strong, and greeted James on the balcony. His crisp white shirt and dark pants were perfect. "So what do you think," I said as I twirled in front of him.

"Diana, you're simply magnificent." We were out of sight of the camera, but still had the listening device to contend with. "So what do you think about Isadora and Nigel?"

"Not sure what they're all about, but they seem like a nice couple."

His next statement could either make or break our undercover operation. "Well, sweetie, I like them a lot. Besides, it sounds like Nigel has a ton of experience with the banking industry here. Plus, the people he introduced me to today seem to be really smart. Maybe they could help us out. We have a lot of money that needs to be invested, and it's not exactly *clean* money."

"You could be right, but let's see how things play out. We don't really need to rush things," I said.

"Oh and by the way, I've decided our room needs an upgrade. I'm having us moved to the penthouse for the rest of our stay."

"You're the best, James. How did I ever get so lucky to find you?"

James was smart. No time for them to bug a new room.

"Must have been karma," he said with a wink.

We left the room and headed to the hotel bar, thankful to be away from cameras and hidden microphones.

31

Smooth Operator,
SADE

Isadora and Nigel were already seated at the bar. She waved me forward, and I took note that her earlier suspicions seemed to have been erased. "You look a little flushed, Diana. Everything okay?"

"Just fine," I answered. Damn, role playing was becoming my forte!

"Well, Nigel and I have been talking," said Isadora. "Sounds like there may be an opportunity for us to work together on that property James has in Florida."

"I'd really like for the two of you to have a good look at it first," James interrupted. "Preferably an on-site visit, then you can give me your advice."

"Well, I'm not sure," Nigel sounded hesitant. "Can't you just take some pictures of the area instead?"

I figured his reluctance had to do with airport customs officers and the fake passports they'd acquired to fly to the Cayman Islands in the first place. Our plan was to get them onto a boat and into international waters or somewhere near the Florida coast. I knew nothing about customs clearance for people who arrived in the US by boat. Presumed the boat could just land anywhere. It's not like in an airport, where you have to get in a line, get scanned, take your shoes off, and have your baggage X-rayed.

"It's worth a few million dollars, and if you help me, perhaps we could consider a partnership?" James maintained a deadpan face. Not giving anything away.

Nigel's demeanour immediately reflected *hook, line, and sinker* mode. Isadora was positively gloating at the amount of money.

"Just one problem," James said. "Diana really hates flying. It took me forever to get her onto a flight to come here in the first place, and the airline almost had to call the paramedics to get her off the plane on a stretcher. I wouldn't want to put her through that again." He wrapped his arm around my shoulder, slightly nudging my ankle. "Our only other option would be by boat, even though it would take longer."

Nigel looked at Isadora. She was busy eyeing the rings on her fingers and probably thinking that with a few more million dollars, she could buy her own jewellery store. She nodded.

"I don't know anyone with a boat. Now it would need to be an oceangoing one," James said. "Do you know anyone?"

Nigel shook his head. "I can check it out."

Isadora smiled. "I may just have a connection on that front. Hang on." Her eyes travelled to the back of the bar. Teddy was just coming on for the evening shift, but squirmed when he saw Isadora again.

"What can I get you ladies . . . and gentlemen?" Teddy asked.

"How about an ocean liner? Know anyone who can get us to Miami? She licked her lips. "We'd make it worth your while."

Teddy looked in my direction, as if to ask, *no charge for the DNA testing or my case?* At least that was my interpretation. I winked.

"Well then, Isadora, you are in luck. My brother has one. In fact, we're headed to Florida tomorrow to pick up some tourists for a return trip. The boat will be pretty much empty on the way there. I'm sure it won't be a problem," Teddy said.

The set-up was perfect. If Nigel and Isadora believed they were finding the boat, instead of us, it would seem a lot less staged or planned. James's phone rang, and he wandered off to take the call. I presumed it was from Randy. Probably already had the scoop on Teddy's brother and was feeding info. Drinks arrived, and I took a sip. Damn, tasted like he'd given me a double. Over my shoulder, I caught James returning with a thumbs-up that only I could see.

Two drinks later, we were set. The boat was leaving at 10:00 a.m. the next morning. Back in the room, I began packing, including all the stuff I'd bought at the psychic's store. James just shook his head.

In the meantime, Randy had already checked out the boat and its owner. "It's all good. Randy knows this guy and has already given him a heads-up," James said.

"It's too easy." I fiddled with the zipper on my suitcase. "It's just that, well, this case hasn't been straightforward from the get-go. Why should everything fall into place now?" I asked.

"Diana, one of the things I've learned is that whatever happens, if things ever get out of sync, you always rise to the challenge."

"Does that mean you trust me, James?"

"Absolutely."

That was all I needed to hear.

32

Love Boat theme song,
JACK JONES

Her name was the *Miss Slipper Bottom*, and from first glance, I was in instant love. She was breathtaking. Massive, long, sleek, graceful lines, not even a mere bob in the water where she was anchored, and that made me feel better, even safe. Flying in an airplane was one thing; me on a boat was quite another. The last time I'd been on the water in a vessel, it resulted in me clinging to the rails and praying for land. This girl, however, looked like she could hold her own, whatever may come. I needed to copy her style.

Maybe I could have left the Gravol behind, but just in case, it was in my palm tree bag along with the pepper spray. According to James, the *Miss Slipper Bottom* had a 121-foot range, with room for ten guests in four staterooms, a Jacuzzi tub on the fly bridge, a garage for an RIB, whatever the heck that was, and two jet skis. Hell, she was five times the size of the apartment I used to rent. Maybe this wouldn't be such a bad deal after all. Fuelling this baby for a two- to three-day trip to Miami probably cost more than my car was worth, even when it was brand new!

James and I, plus the crew, had purposely arrived early. James briefed Teddy and his brother with a few details. Not enough to compromise the takedown, but just enough to give them the drift. All were in agreement, and I nodded at Teddy. "Yup, no charge for your case."

Randy was on board as the pseudo chef. Had a real chef as a backup, and one of his staff was prepared to act as the maid. Teddy was the onboard maître d' and bartender, which meant this would definitely be a booze cruise. I figured the more liquor that flowed the easier it would be on all of us. And then there was James. Wow, couldn't have asked for anything better—in his T-shirt and shorts, he was a total hunk. Randy looked like a linebacker for the NFL, and yikes, now there was Teddy and his brother, who was his spitting image, except for the official captain's attire, including the hat and some gold bars on the sleeve of his white tight-fitting jacket. If ever I was going to be stranded on an island, this would totally represent my top list of men to have.

Isadora rolled her Louis Vuitton suitcase up the ramp, looking a tad hung over. Good, maybe that would keep her out of my hair for a while. We had fifteen minutes to settle in before departure and the required safety lecture. Nigel and the guys were rambling on about 15 knots top-end and 13 knots cruise speed, a 3,400 nautical mile range, when I zoned out. All I really needed to know was where the lifejackets were, while keeping tabs on which man was closest in case I needed to grab him. At this point, it was definitely James first, Randy and Teddy would tie for a close second, and Teddy's brother would be third. If it came to Nigel, I reckoned I'd be better off on my own.

It seemed the guys were letting Nigel guide the conversation. Great, he'd feel like he was in charge. Most times, it's all about power and control and who has it, or in this case, who *thinks* he has it. If Nigel felt like he was on the right side of any decision-making, it was because it meshed with the pre-planning. I, on the other hand, knew better. The other guys were way ahead of him.

Champagne flowed as we pulled out of the harbour. Turquoise water, light breeze, sun shining—it was perfect. Too perfect, and I wasn't sure if it was the *Love Boat* theme song that ran through my head or my recollections of the craft featured on the *Gilligan's Island* TV series that was responsible for the itch in the middle of my back. Mind you, if I was going to be stranded, I had the right team of guys to handle that. Still, I had the feeling that somewhere along the line this whole venture would turn out to be "hell in a hand basket," as my mother would say.

...

We'd been at sea for a couple of days, motored into international waters, and according to James, things were going well. He and Randy decided we'd wait until we were closer to the Florida shore to apprehend them. It would be easier in US waters since the crime had been committed in the States. The coast guard was on alert, and all seemed to be going better than planned. Isadora and Nigel spent a lot of time in the hot tub, which I refused to enter. Shades of Andrew and that whole scene at the couples retreat were still rampant in my mind. Besides, I noticed that bathing suits didn't seem to be a required commodity for these two. Hell, even Teddy shielded his eyes when he left a stack of towels and a couple of bathrobes draped over the Jacuzzi.

Instead, I lay on a deck chair, tanning and purposefully looking at the sun, hoping for temporary blindness in case the two of them decided to stroll my way, after exiting the hot tub, without their robes. "It's okay," James said to me. "You're playing it well."

"How much longer will it take?" I asked.

"We should be able to wrap it up by tomorrow. By then, we'll be just a few hours off the coast of Miami, so close enough."

This provided some assurance, but not enough. The itch in my back intensified, and I struggled to reach the spot, wishing for longer arms or one of those back scratchers I'd seen at the Dollar Store.

...

The next day we were about three hours off the Miami coast, enjoying a lunch of lobster rolls, a green salad, and some tequila-based cocktails on the upper deck. I still couldn't shake the feeling that a storm was about to unleash, even though the sun shone and skies were cloudless. James and Nigel sorted through some documents while Isadora and I maintained a somewhat superficial conversation. The damned itch was back, and I stood up to get away from the irritating couple who were inciting it. No such luck. Isadora followed a few feet behind, carrying her drink.

"Sorry, my darling Diana," James said. "I know how business stuff bores you."

I saw the look on James's face after the words were out of his mouth. Something along the lines of, *Oh shit. What have I done?*

Isadora did an immediate about-face, looked at James, then at Nigel and back at me. The use of my first and last name had connected the dots. Isadora's face displayed shock, then horror, and oh yes, anger, including rage-filled bulging eyes. She resembled a kewpie doll that had been squeezed too tight around the neck. Since the only weapon in her hand was the cocktail, I figured I could handle her throwing a drink at me. That was until she broke the glass against an umbrella stand and faced me. The base of the glass was clutched in her fist. The shard poked between her fingers and looked worthy of serious personal damage.

I also knew that when women fight it's a whole lot different than men. Men tend to square off, put some space between them, do the eye to eye thing, raise their fists, and duke it out. Women are more like cats fighting. No holds barred. Hair pulling, biting, scratching, and even a bit of hissing and spitting were a given. But here was this lady, with a glass shard in her hand, heading my way.

"You sonovabitch," she shrieked. "You're that PI I hired. Knew I recognized your voice. You're the one the psychic warned me about. You're done." She charged towards me. I took a few steps back, set myself into a somewhat crouching stance, and prepared to tackle her.

Out of the corner of my eye, I caught a glimpse of Nigel as he attempted a bow-legged lumber after Isadora. James easily got ahead and gave Nigel one of those clothesline throttles I'd seen in wrestling shows. Apparently a full arm across the neck works, and Nigel was down like a sack of shit, but still struggling.

Isadora's sandals skittered and slipped on the deck as she ran at me. I hoped and prayed she'd fall. No such luck. The railing pressed hard against my back. No escaping. She picked up speed. At the very last second, I ducked, pleased that the glass shard had been avoided. Forward momentum carried her body hurtling over the rail in a mass of flailing arms, kicking legs, and an orange floor-length wraparound skirt that now encircled her neck. It looked like a long way down.

"Can't swim," Isadora's words drifted up to me.

"Don't go after her," James shouted. "I'll get Randy."

It was too late to heed the warning. The last thing I wanted to do was be responsible for a death by drowning. Besides, I knew the A-team was on board, and surely they would muster. I stood on the railing and dove into the water.

Down, down, down I went. Cripes, how tall was this damned boat? It was taking forever. The water's entry slowed the force, but still down I went, finally bottomed out, turned, and got my head above my feet. Now, where was she? My eyes opened. There was a sting from the sea salt.

Then, nothing. Just clear ocean with no flailing arms or legs in sight. After a 360-degree pivot in the water, she was still nowhere in sight. I needed air and went back to the surface. A head of hair floated a few feet away. Perfect! I grabbed it, relieved that I'd rescued her, and it had been so easy. Shit, it was a damned wig. Why hadn't I picked up on that before? Now I knew why her hair was so consistently coiffed.

Sirens were blaring on the *Miss Slipper Bottom*, although I'm not sure why. We were alone in the water. It's not like you could call 911 and paramedics would rush in. My last glimpse of the boat was James diving overboard. Down I went again. This time I saw Isadora. The orange skirt was hard to miss, and she was still kicking. Good, she was alive. I'd get her to the surface and wait for the guys. I grabbed her shoulders. Her eyes were wide open, filled with a mixture of panic and anger. Not a good combination. She nailed me in the stomach with her knee as we rose up. Okay, sometimes I can be a forgiving soul, but then again, maybe not. I chose to believe it was accidental.

I struggled to get her to the surface. We'd both swallowed a lot of water and gasped for air. She opened her mouth and spewed out water. A sound of air erupted from her lungs and reminded me of burping Tupperware. Thin grey hair plastered her head. No wonder she wore a wig. Gaping lips and jowls that opened and closed reminded me of a fish out of water. I resisted the urge to give an undercut blow to the chin as payback for the kick. Instead, since she was reasonably compliant, I held back. Took a moment to look up at the sky and mentally thanked Mom for making me take those damned lifeguarding classes during summers as a teen.

Cripes, what was this? Something prickly was creeping up my leg. I kicked the offender, hoping it wasn't a jellyfish, an octopus, or even worse a shark fin. The prickling continued up my leg—I was having one of those eureka moments.

A head with a crew cut bobbed above the surface. It was James. If I didn't already have one arm around Isadora to keep her afloat, I'd have cheerfully thrown both arms around him.

"Geez, Diana, what in hell were you thinking?" James asked.

I smiled. "Guess I wasn't. You know me too well."

Isadora chose that moment to resubmerge. Or maybe it was the fact I'd just let my grip on her slip. James had her back on the surface in an instant. His arms around her, and I was jealous. "Fuck you," she spluttered.

"Right back at ya!" he said. "My sentiments exactly."

"Hang on, Diana. Help is on the way," James said.

I caught the rear of the *Miss Slipper Bottom* still motoring away and wondered how much time it would to take a boat of that size to slow down, or even worse turn around. What kind of help was he talking about? That's when I heard the roaring sound of engines as if something was in full speed, coming closer. It looked like an inflatable raft but obviously well-powered. Randy was at the helm. James waved and gave a thumbs-up salute as the craft slowed to a bobbing stop beside us.

"You guys okay?" Randy asked.

"Never better, take her first," James said, pointing at Isadora.

"Well, if I had my druthers, I'd be going for Diana first," he grinned as he hauled Isadora over the side of the raft. Her skirt was helping restrict her leg movements, and she fell to the bottom of the boat. "Look at this lady, already wearing the required orange prison jumpsuit."

I was next and welcomed the relief of the strong arms that pulled me from the water and up over the side. Then, I made sure I was safely in the rear of the craft and far away from Isadora.

"James, you can do this on your own?" Randy asked.

"Trust me, buddy. That was a given." He'd already straddled the side of the craft and was upright. "So where's Nigel at?"

"No worries. Teddy's got him strapped to a rail by the Jacuzzi tub and is standing guard. Teddy's brother has already been in contact with the coast guard, and they'll meet us halfway. This is going better than planned except for the overboard hiccup."

Huh, I was thinking. *He considered this just a hiccup? If life-threatening scenarios like this didn't scare these guys, I hesitated to wonder what in hell it would take!* I felt like I was being left out. James eyed me.

"Awesome job, Diana. Knew I could count on you. But I gotta ask, when I told you not to jump overboard, what on God's green earth were you thinking?" James asked.

I hesitated. No immediate answer came to mind. I glanced at the sky. Mom was there. This time there was no message. I'd have to do this on my own.

"Guess I was just doing what I thought was right at the time."

33

A Hard Day's Night,
THE BEATLES

At long last, we were back on land. If the guys hadn't been there, I'd have cheerfully knelt down and kissed the ground. Instead, I chose to keep up the *strong woman* persona they seemed to have bestowed upon me. Hell, Randy had even referred to me as *woman warrior*. Wow, what a compliment! Teddy's brother mentioned something about getting me on a slow boat to China, whatever the heck that meant, and Teddy just looked at me with admiration. James's silence was deafening, and I hated it. Damn him. He'd gotten under my skin. The itch in my back had returned, and I wondered what was going through his mind.

The coast guard had relieved us of Nigel and Isadora, and my last glimpse of them was being led away in handcuffs. Since they both seemed to enjoy the Velcro type, I wondered how they'd deal with cold hard metal instead.

James finally pulled me aside. "Okay, so I've got a lot of paperwork to do before they get arraigned before a judge. I've arranged for a car to take you home, and I'll let you know the court date."

Huh, that was it? Over and done just like that, in spite of all we'd been through together. Had I totally misjudged this guy? My stomach churned, my hackles rose, and I desperately wanted to take a swing at him with my fist. Damn him. Instead I waited, calmed down, even managed to keep my mouth shut. Maybe I was learning some lessons here about third chances in life. At least this time, I hadn't struck out entirely.

"For sure, James. No problem, just keep me posted," I said.

"Thanks for understanding." He turned and walked away. I stared at his back. Waiting for him to turn around, give me a look, or maybe a wave. Nothing, and I was heartbroken.

...

Meanwhile, back at the office, I did a crash and burn. Slept for a solid eight hours and woke up with a crick in my neck. The smell of freshly brewed coffee drew me to the photocopy room where I found Bambi lining up cat treats on a little silver serving tray while Xena inhaled them one at a time.

"So how's business?" I asked.

Bambi whirled around and said, "Good Lord, girl. You look like death warmed over!"

Since I hadn't checked myself in the mirror, she could be right. Bambi threw her arms around my neck and gave me a solid hug. The hug and coffee were exactly what I needed in the moment.

"Come with me." She grabbed my hand and led me to the front of the office. "Everything. I want to hear everything. Right down to the last detail. So is he any good in bed?"

"Can't say." I shrugged.

"So does that mean it didn't happen, or does it mean you're not telling?" Bambi asked.

"Both," I said with a wink. "Now what I can say is that your ex-husband, Nigel, and his accomplice, Isadora, are safely behind bars."

"Oh My God," she shrieked, hugged me again, and planted a kiss on my cheek. "You're the best! More details, Diana, I need more."

We spent the next hour emptying the coffee pot while I recounted everything from the flight, the forced teaming sting operation with Randy, and the trip home. By the time I finished, her eyes were bulging, even though I left out the lovemaking scenario and the trip to the psychic. Gotta admit, it felt good to unload on listening ears that seemed to understand.

"Anyways, what about business?" I asked.

"Well, like I said earlier, the kid isn't Teddy's. I found Deborah's sister living in Reno, Nevada. Think they're going to hook up in the next week or two. As for Dave and his encounter with the pumpkin, I'll leave that one up to you."

I nodded. After the last few days, perhaps investigating a pumpkin festival might not be a bad idea, even if it was a tad boring. At least it would be safer.

"Plus I've been plowing through the online PI course materials. Almost done and should be taking the final exam by the end of the month. I think you should take me on as a partner."

Huh, what was Bambi thinking?

"Let's be honest here. It's not like you've got a crowd beating down your door for business. I've seen your files, and they're kind of meagre," she said.

The phone rang. Bambi looked down, grabbed it on the first ring, and gave the required preamble. "Yes, of course, Melanie. I'll inform Ms. Darling regarding the time and place." She hung up and grinned. "Looks like the arraignment is tomorrow. I wouldn't miss this for the world. Oh, and by the way, I took the liberty of adding call display. That crazy lady, Nikki, just keeps calling, and this way I can avoid her. Who is she anyways?"

"What does she say when she calls?" I asked.

"Mostly that she's in trouble. Rambles on about someone named Jimmie. Demands to speak with you and says it's your fault," Bambi said.

Yikes, looked like Nikki wasn't going away. "Well that would be James's ex-wife. It's complicated, and I can't explain more right now. Just try to listen and let her rant a bit," I said.

Bambi rolled her eyes as if to question, but she chose not to.

...

It was the next day, and I was in a courtroom for the initial hearing on Nigel and Isadora's case. A first for me, and I welcomed Bambi's presence next to me in the back row. Harold was beside her and looked a few inches taller than I remembered him being. That's when I realized he was sitting on one of those inflatable ring donuts. Guess being shot in the butt can be a real pain in the ass and takes time to resolve. The seats in front of us were filled with ten seniors who were alleged victims of Nigel and Isadora's money scam.

Snippets of conversation filtered back: *"Can't believe I was taken in by that jerk. What kind of guy rips us off like that? He deserves to rot in hell. I'm no lawyer, but I say we consider a class-action lawsuit?"* The row in front was nodding like a collective group of bobblehead dolls.

The side door opened as Nigel and Isadora were led in. No handcuffs this time. Seems to have been replaced with leg shackles. Bulky orange prison jumpsuits didn't look bad on either of them. Kind of matched the colour of Nigel's hair. Isadora, on the other hand, looked like she'd aged. Or maybe it was the sparse grey tendrils of hair that clung to her skull. Plus she was there minus the makeup. Guess they didn't sell wigs or lipstick in prison.

Then, a commanding voice came from the front of the room. "All rise. The Honourable Judge Judy Henry will be presiding. Creaking noises from hip and knee joints came from the row in front as they stood. Cripes, James was still absent. I couldn't believe he'd miss this. The judge entered the room. Holy crap, she was dressed in a black flowing robe, had a lace collar around her neck, and a no-nonsense look about her. Even I would not have dared lying in front of her.

The back door whispered open, and James slid into the seat beside me. *Sorry to be late*, he mouthed. Passed an envelope my way that read "open later."

Judge Judy Henry banged the gavel. "Court is now in session. Let's hear the first case."

The prosecutor rose and listed a series of charges laid against Isadora and Nigel. James's presence left me totally distracted and unable to focus on the mumbo jumbo legal talk that was being presented. A quick glance revealed nothing. No emotion as he stared straight ahead. It made me wonder, who was this guy and had I totally misjudged him? Especially after all we'd just been through. Two could play this game. There was no way I'd be anything less than professional, so I stared ahead and tried to ignore the scent of Old Spice.

The lawyer for the defence stood and entered a plea of *not guilty on all counts*. Even had the audacity to request bail. Judge Judy Henry rolled her eyes, peered over her glasses, and stared him down. "Denied," she banged the gavel. "The court will set a date for a hearing. Bring on the next case."

I was so close to James that I felt the vibration of the cell phone in his pocket. Once he heard the word *denied*, he was gone. In the end, Nigel and Isadora were charged with fraud. No bail since they already exhumed a couple of bodies, fled the country, and were considered a flight risk. Great, they were headed back to jail. Legalities would at least take a couple of years while the Cayman Islands bank accounts were totally investigated. I searched for James in the parking lot. He was nowhere in sight. Tires and testicles be damned—Mom had been right again!

34

On the Road Again,
WILLIE NELSON

Back at the office, I tore open the envelope from James. Holy shit, it was a cheque for ten thousand dollars for services rendered and for going above and beyond, according to the brief note that accompanied it. I spent the next few days deciding on a course of action including how and where to spend it. The owner of the strip mall dropped by to pick up the monthly rent and mentioned the apartment above my office was for available. Asked if I was interested and said it was just basic, but since it had a real bedroom, a real kitchen, and holy shit, an actual bathroom with a tub and shower, instead of a janitor's closet with plumbing, I took it without seeing it. Besides, Xena would have an even higher view of the parking lot.

In the meantime, there was still no word from James. I refused to be the first to call. Besides, I had plenty on my plate and made a critical decision. Bambi was about to become my new business partner.

It was hard to believe that only a few short weeks ago I'd set up the Diana Darling Private Investigator Agency. Since then, I almost learned how to shoot a gun, went undercover at a couples retreat, visited a seniors strip club, may have been the cause of its burning demise, witnessed a church shooting, hired a receptionist, saved the life of James (a real private detective), met his crazy ex-wife, went dumpster diving, took down three bad guys (well two men and one woman to be exact), travelled to the Cayman Islands, dove overboard on the *Miss Slipper Bottom* en route to Miami to rescue the *bad* woman, went to court, AND met the hottest guy I've ever encountered in my life.

Now came the aftermath, the letdown, and wondering how my life would ever be the same. Bottom line, it wouldn't. I sat at my desk, fingered the business card that read *James R. Woods*, and flipped it over to display the private number written on the back. To call or not to call, that was the question. Actually it was more like an internal mind debate. I'd saved his life but since he'd also saved mine, I reckoned the score was even.

We'd kept it strictly business for the most part, and the last thing I wanted to do was come across as a less-than-professional PI, or even worse as a desperate woman in need of a man. I'd also grown up in an era where you waited for the guy to make the first move—pretty damned antiquated etiquette by today's standards.

Xena leapt onto my desk. Now I'm no cat whisperer, but I swear her soulful eyes were saying *call him*. She even put her paw on the receiver. "Message received," I murmured whilst stroking the top of her head with my fingers.

I was about to pick up the phone when she parked herself over it. Damn cat, was getting in the way. That's when it rang. Thanks to my recently acquired call display feature, I knew it was him. Let it ring three times before picking up. No need to pinch the nose this time and pretend to be a receptionist. Xena's tail swished back and forth like a metronome. Timing was everything. I took in a deep breath, exhaled, and guided my voice towards sounding nonchalant, or so I hoped.

"Yes, James, how can I help you?" I asked.

"Any chance you're up for another case?" James asked.

I settled back in my chair, propped my legs up on the desk, and made him wait before responding, "Well, that depends. I'm kind of busy with new clients."

His chuckle on the phone reminded me that this guy could read me like a book. Hopefully it was a one of those mystery books with a really intricate plot line, where he'd at least have to work at it, but true to form, my tongue overrode my brain. So much for practice.

Instead I blurted out, "On the other hand, I could be enticed . . . if the price is right. And I will require more specific details before proceeding."

"Trust me, Diana Darling, the good news is that it will pay well once the case is resolved."

"So if that's the good news, then why do I feel like there's bad news coming?"

"Well, it will require another flight, and I know how you feel about being on an airplane." He paused. "Ever been to Las Vegas?"

New York may be touted as the city that never sleeps, but believe me, Vegas is a 24/7 operation and definitely branded as Sin City for a reason. I didn't think it was the right time to tell him I'd married my second ex-husband there at one of those quickie wedding chapels where the so-called minister was an Elvis Presley look-alike. When I went back a few hours later to see if he could tear up the marriage certificate, he'd already left the building.

Holy crap, another trip! I ran my fingers through my hair and leaned back in my chair. Xena was eyeing the cat treat drawer as if she'd just scored a home run for guiding me on the right course of action, timing included.

"So, James, I presume you'll be covering the extra expenses, including any required wardrobe?"

He chuckled, "Trust me, I know you, Diana. That was already a given."

"Plus, I'll need a deposit to cover any loss of income while I'm away."

"Diana, you can consider it done. Pack your bags and I'll pick you up at 9:00 a.m."

"In that case, Sin City here we come."

...

The next morning, I was packed and sitting in my office when a car sped into the parking lot. Tires squealed, and the car screeched to a stop in front of my door. Cripes, it was James and an hour early. What the hell was going on? He raced into the office, grabbed my bags, and threw them in the trunk of the car. Flung open the passenger door and shouted, "Quick, get in."

I was barely in the seat before he took off. I had a million questions, but the look on his face was enough to signal that now was not the right time. After what seemed an eternity, he faced me.

"Have you heard from Nikki?" James asked.

I wrestled with remaining calm. "Well, Bambi said she'd called the office a few times. Sounded a bit frantic and was asking for you. Why?"

"She called me during the night. Said she was in trouble and that she'd been kidnapped. Also mentioned your name and something about blood."

Holy shit, no wonder his face looked so tense. "So now what, James?" I asked.

"Can't leave town until I'm sure she's okay. Sorry to involve you in my personal stuff, but I could really use your help. Besides, if you're with me, I'll know you're safe," James said.

His face was starting to look less intense, more focused.

"Of course, James, we are a team you know."

Silence. Then, finally he responded, "That we are, Diana Darling. That we are."

The End

CPSIA information can be obtained
at www.ICGtesting.com
Printed in the USA
LVHW042246270821
696290LV00010B/745

9 781039 111370